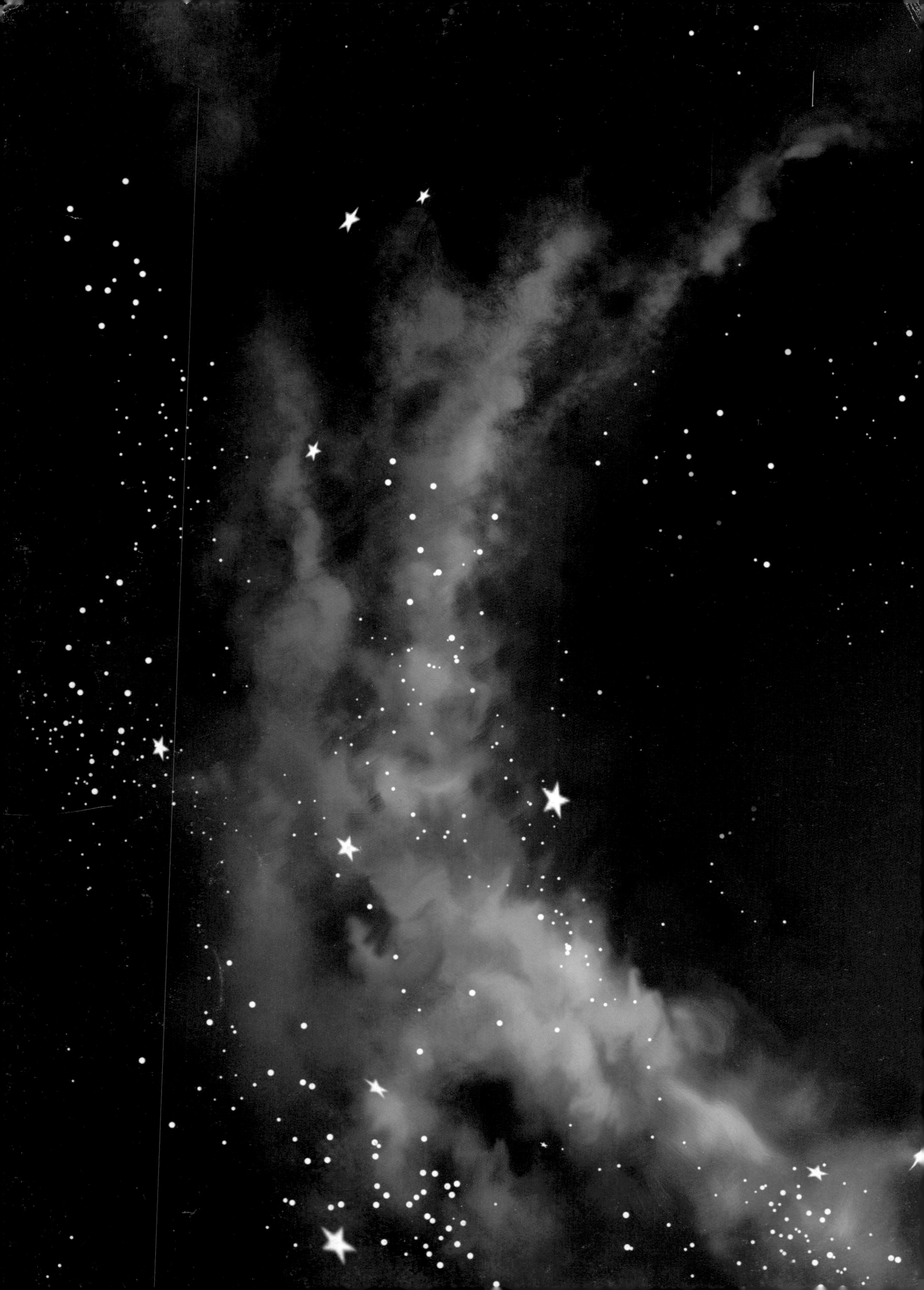

My dear Rose,

On the Planet of the Tear-Eaters, I observed not only the pain of having one's work overlooked by others but also the joy of sharing one's creations with friends.

Art in all its forms has the tremendous power of enriching life through the creation of beauty. And beauty shared is beauty multiplied, like a single seed that blooms into a meadow of flowers.

During my voyages, I have shared many beautiful moments with new friends, but my dearest wish has always been to share them with you when I see you again at last.

The Little Prince

First American edition published in 2014 by Graphic Universe™.

Le Petit Prince™

based on the masterpiece by Antoine de Saint-Exupéry

© 2014 LPPM
An animated series based on the novel Le Petit Prince by Antoine de Saint-Exupéry
Developed for television by Matthieu Delaporte, Alexandre de la Patellière, and Bertrand Gatignol
Directed by Pierre-Alain Chartier

© 2014 ÉDITIONS GLÉNAT
Copyright © 2014 by Lerner Publishing Group, Inc., for the current edition

Graphic Universe™
A division of Lerner Publishing Group, Inc.
241 First Avenue North
Minneapolis, MN 55401 U.S.A.

For reading levels and more information, look up this title at www.lernerbooks.com.

Library of Congress Cataloging-in-Publication Data

Bruneau, Clotilde
  [Planète du grand bouffon. English]
  The planet of the grand buffoon / story by Matteo Cerami, Vincenzo Cerami, and Thierry Gaudin ; design and illustrations by Elyum Studio ; adaptation by Clotilde Bruneau ; translation, Anne Collins Smith and Owen Smith.
     p.   cm. — (The little prince ; #14)
  ISBN 978-0-7613-8764-0 (lib. bdg. : alk. paper)
  ISBN 978-1-4677-2424-1 (eBook)
  1. Graphic novels. I. Cerami, Matteo. II. Cerami, Vincenzo, 1940- III. Gaudin, Thierry. IV. Smith, Anne Collins, translator. V. Smith, Owen (Owen M.), translator. VI. Saint-Exupéry, Antoine de, 1900-1944. Petit Prince. VII. Elyum Studio. VIII. Petit Prince (Television program) IX. Title.
PZ7.7.B8Plg 2014
741.5'944—dc23   2013014885

Manufactured in the United States of America
1 — VI — 12/31/13

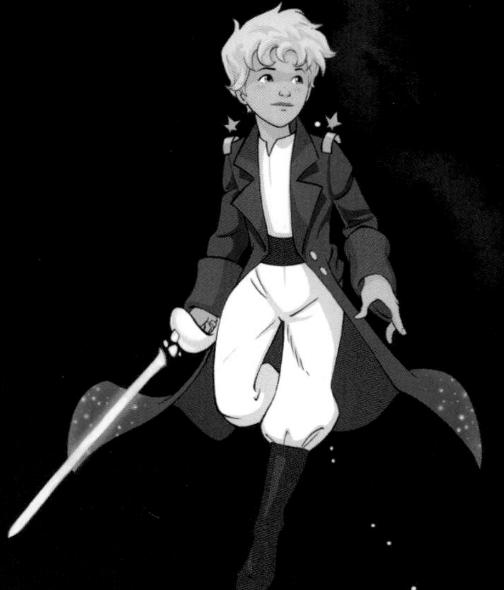

THE NEW ADVENTURES
BASED ON THE MASTERPIECE BY ANTOINE DE SAINT-EXUPÉRY

The Little Prince

The Planet of the Grand Buffoon

Based on the animated series and an original story by Matteo Cerami, Vincenzo Cerami, and Thierry Gaudin

Design: Elyum Studio
Story: Clotilde Bruneau
Artistic Direction: Didier Poli
Art: Audrey Bussi
Backgrounds: Clara Karunakara-Chardavoine
Coloring: Karine Lambin & Digikore
Editing: Olivier Schramm
Editorial Consultant: Didier Convard

Translation: Anne and Owen Smith

Graphic Universe™ • Minneapolis

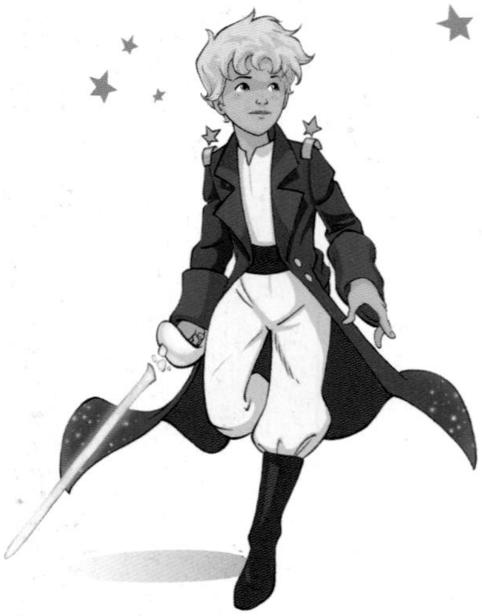

★ THE LITTLE PRINCE

The Little Prince has extraordinary gifts. His sense of wonder allows him to discover what no one else can see. The Little Prince can communicate with all the beings in the universe, even the animals and plants. His powers grow over the course of his adventures.

The Prince's uniform:
When he transforms into the uniform of a prince, he is more agile and quick. When faced with difficult situations, the Little Prince also uses a sword that lets him sketch and bring to life anything from his imagination.

His sketchbook:
When he is not in his Prince's clothing, the Little Prince carries a sketchbook. When he blows on the pages, they take wing and form objects that he'll find very useful. Like his sword, it's powered by stardust collected on his travels.

★ FOX

A grouch, a trickster, and, so he says, interested only in his next meal, Fox is in reality the Little Prince's best friend. As such, he is always there to give him help but also just as much to help him to grow and to learn about the world.

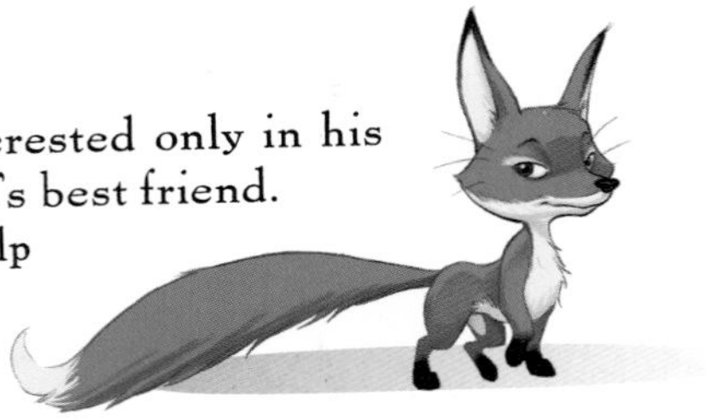

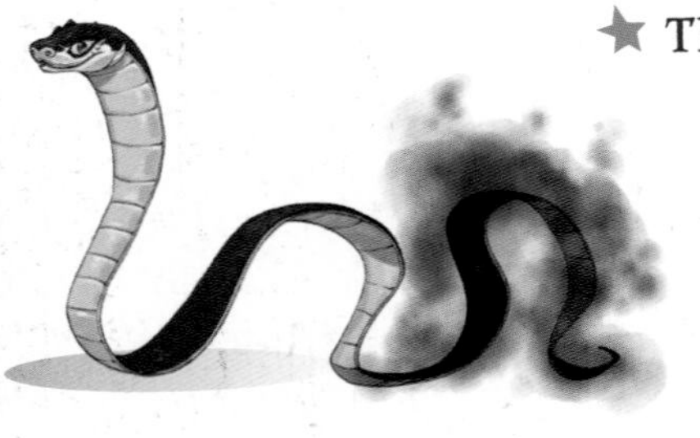

★ THE SNAKE

Even though the Little Prince still does not know exactly why, there can be no doubt that the Snake has set his mind to plunging the entire universe into darkness! And to accomplish his goal, this malicious being is ready to use any form of deception. However, the Snake never takes action himself. He prefers to bring out the wickedness in those beings he has chosen to bite, tempting them to put their own worlds in danger.

★ THE GLOOMIES

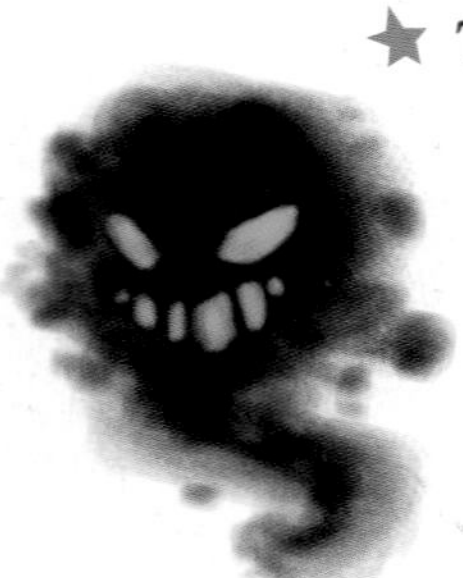

When people who have been "bitten" by the Snake have completely destroyed their own planets, they become Gloomies, slaves to their Snake master. The Gloomies act as a group and carry out the Snake's most vile orders so he can get the better of the Little Prince!

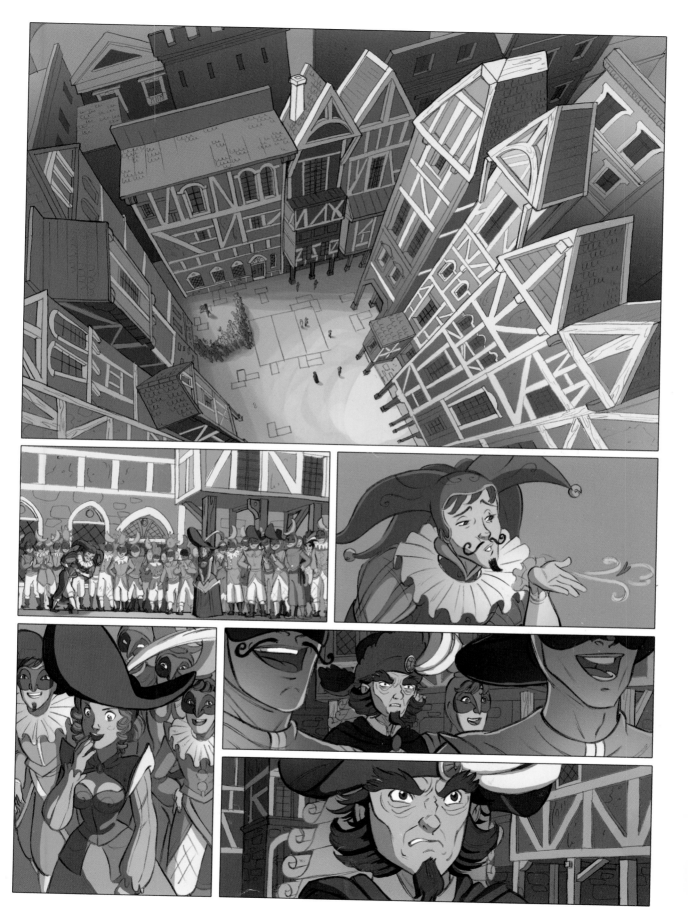

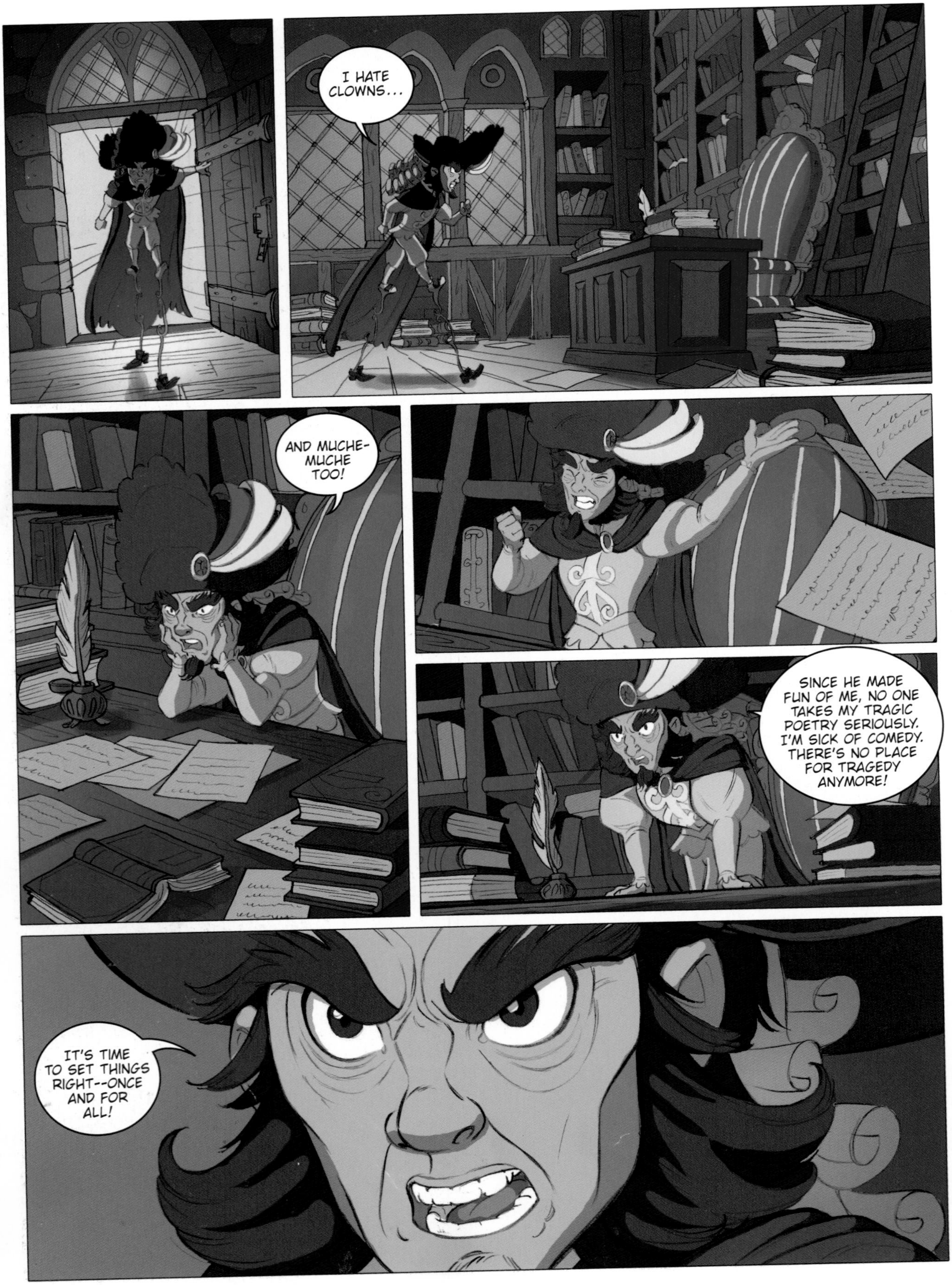
I HATE CLOWNS...
AND MUCHE-MUCHE TOO!
SINCE HE MADE FUN OF ME, NO ONE TAKES MY TRAGIC POETRY SERIOUSLY. I'M SICK OF COMEDY. THERE'S NO PLACE FOR TRAGEDY ANYMORE!
IT'S TIME TO SET THINGS RIGHT--ONCE AND FOR ALL!

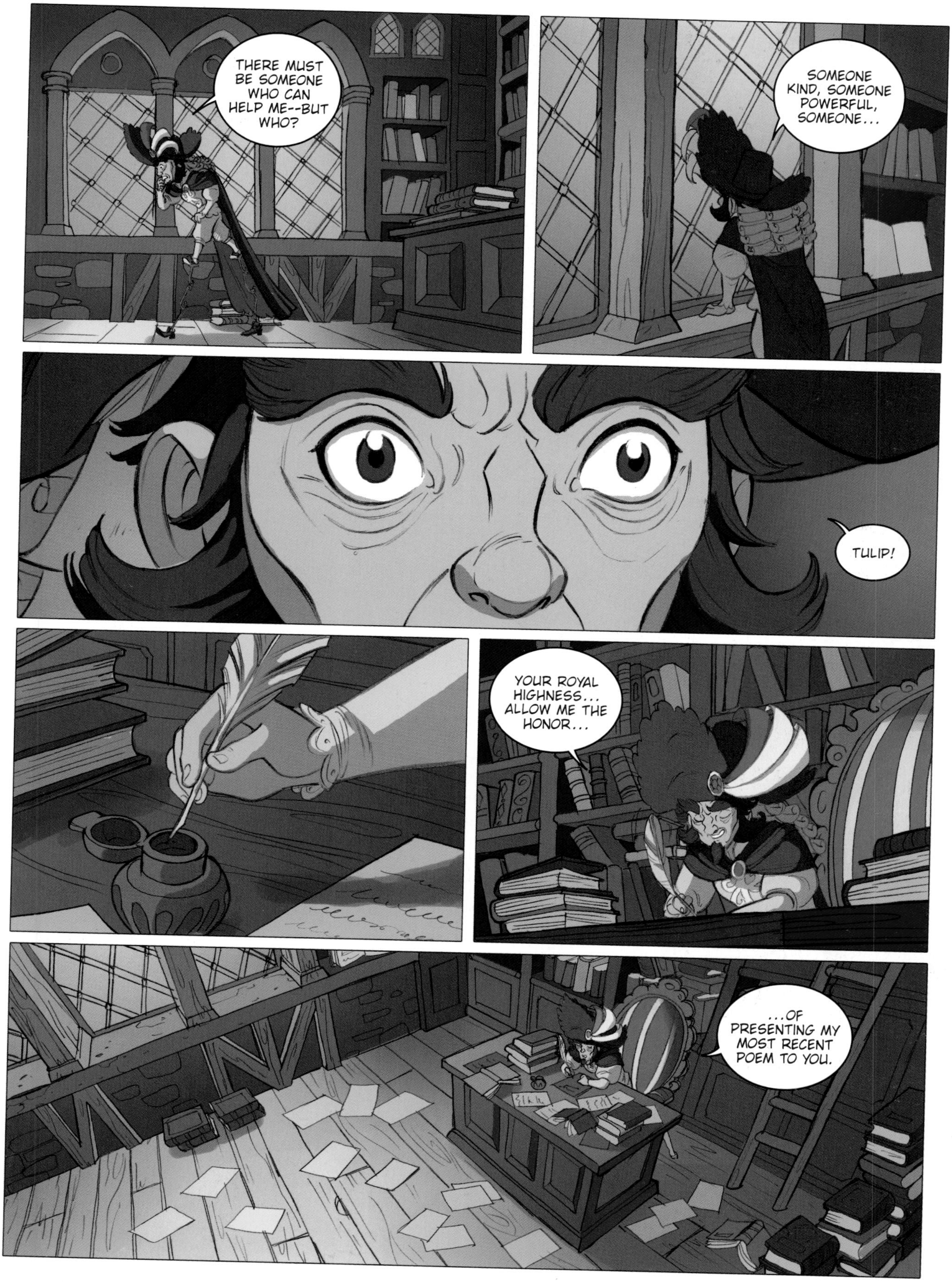
THERE MUST BE SOMEONE WHO CAN HELP ME--BUT WHO?
SOMEONE KIND, SOMEONE POWERFUL, SOMEONE...
TULIP!
YOUR ROYAL HIGHNESS... ALLOW ME THE HONOR...
...OF PRESENTING MY MOST RECENT POEM TO YOU.

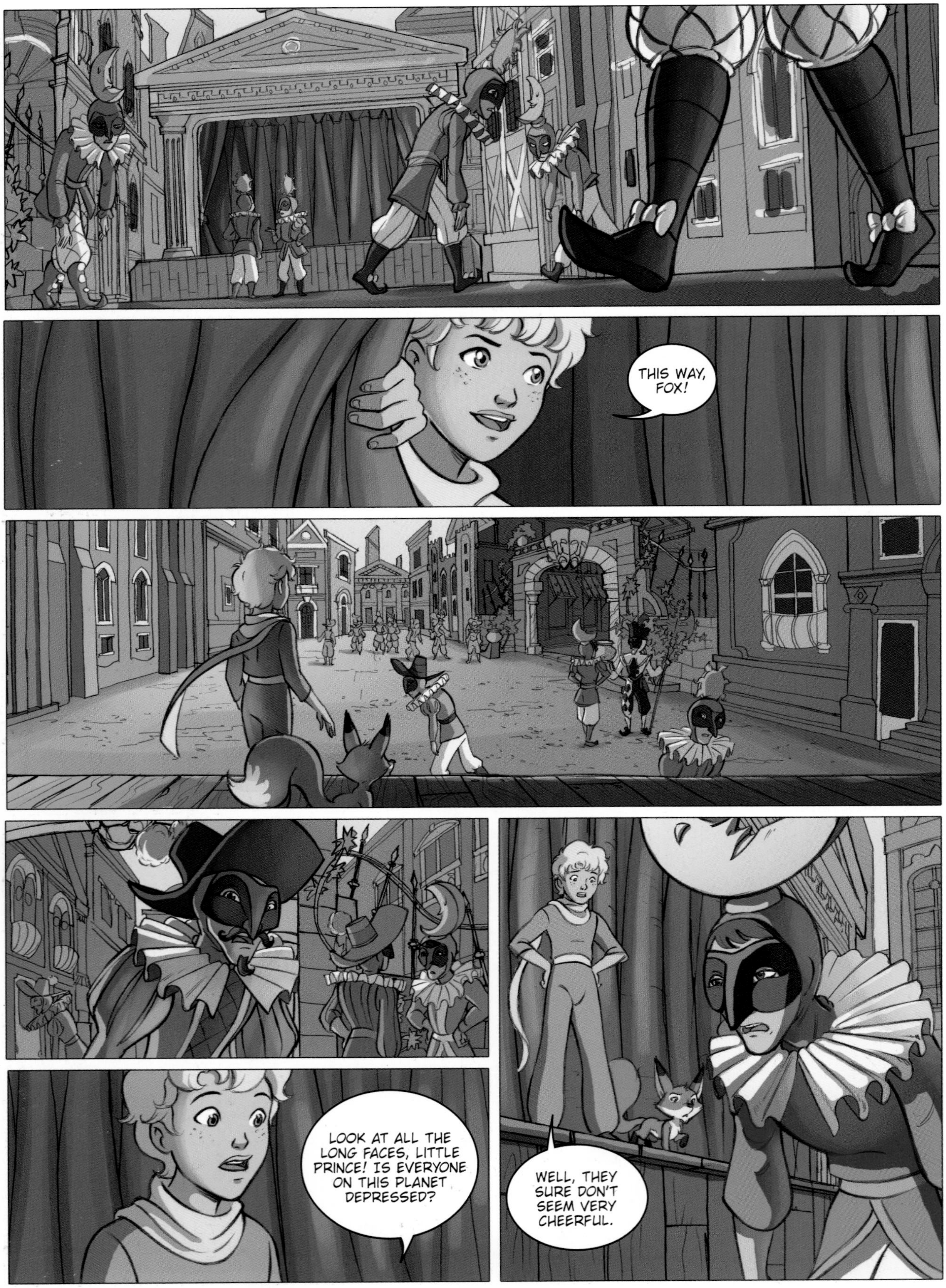
THIS WAY, FOX!
LOOK AT ALL THE LONG FACES, LITTLE PRINCE! IS EVERYONE ON THIS PLANET DEPRESSED?
WELL, THEY SURE DON'T SEEM VERY CHEERFUL.

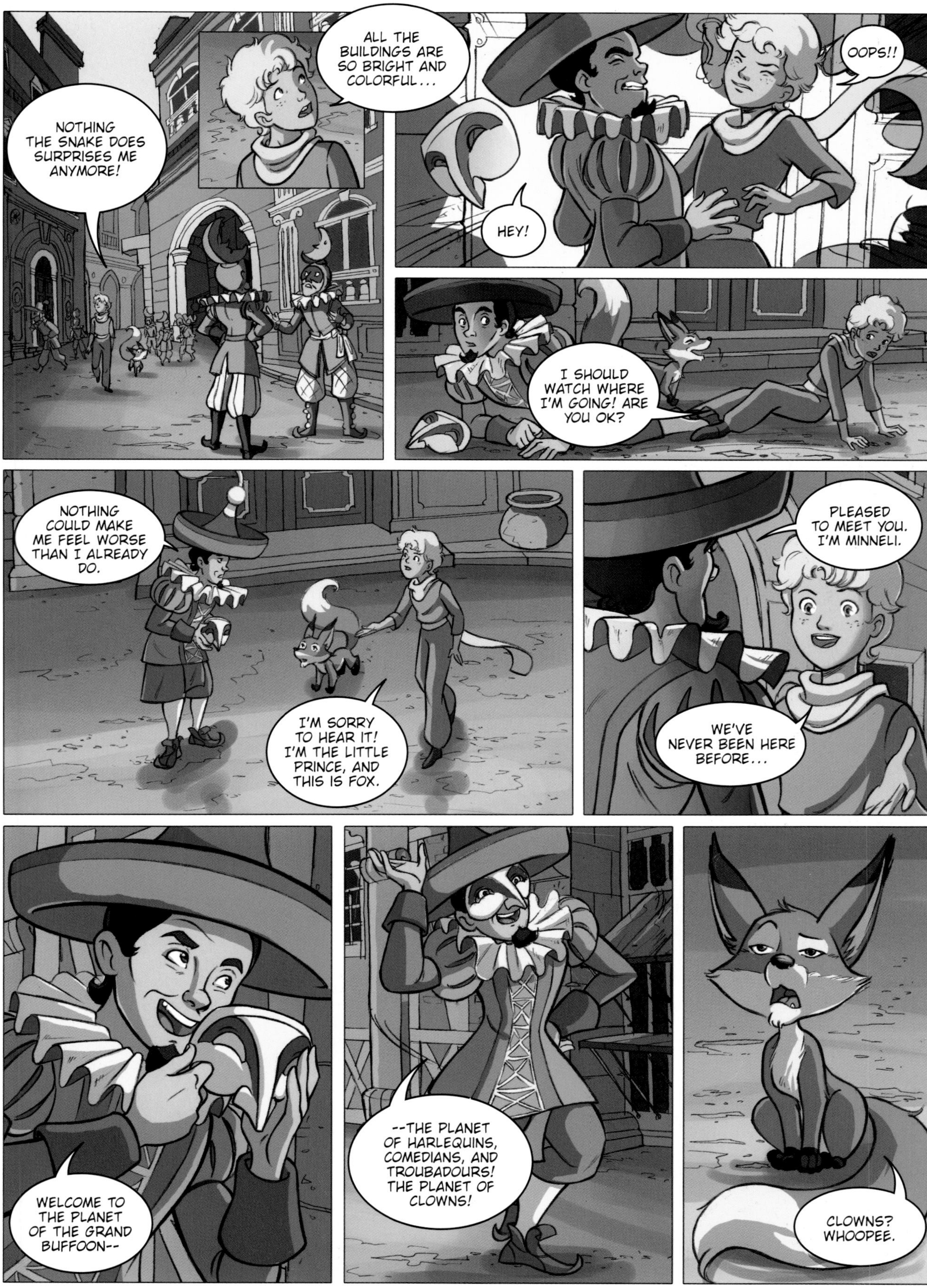
ALL THE BUILDINGS ARE SO BRIGHT AND COLORFUL...
NOTHING THE SNAKE DOES SURPRISES ME ANYMORE!
OOPS!!
HEY!
I SHOULD WATCH WHERE I'M GOING! ARE YOU OK?
NOTHING COULD MAKE ME FEEL WORSE THAN I ALREADY DO.
I'M SORRY TO HEAR IT! I'M THE LITTLE PRINCE, AND THIS IS FOX.
PLEASED TO MEET YOU. I'M MINNELI.
WE'VE NEVER BEEN HERE BEFORE...
WELCOME TO THE PLANET OF THE GRAND BUFFOON--
--THE PLANET OF HARLEQUINS, COMEDIANS, AND TROUBADOURS! THE PLANET OF CLOWNS!
CLOWNS? WHOOPEE.

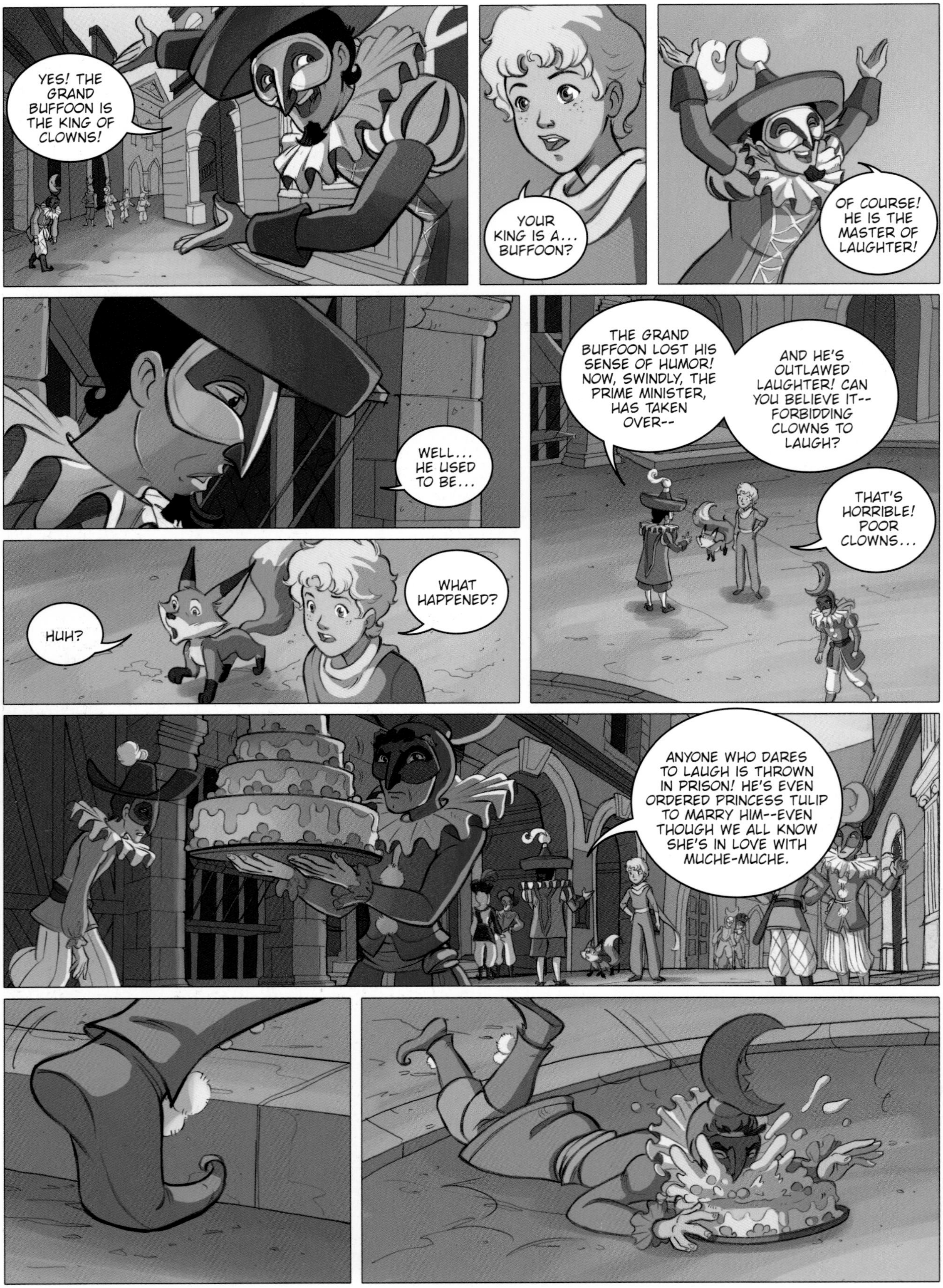

YES! THE GRAND BUFFOON IS THE KING OF CLOWNS!
YOUR KING IS A... BUFFOON?
OF COURSE! HE IS THE MASTER OF LAUGHTER!
WELL... HE USED TO BE...
HUH?
WHAT HAPPENED?
THE GRAND BUFFOON LOST HIS SENSE OF HUMOR! NOW, SWINDLY, THE PRIME MINISTER, HAS TAKEN OVER--
AND HE'S OUTLAWED LAUGHTER! CAN YOU BELIEVE IT--FORBIDDING CLOWNS TO LAUGH?
THAT'S HORRIBLE! POOR CLOWNS...
ANYONE WHO DARES TO LAUGH IS THROWN IN PRISON! HE'S EVEN ORDERED PRINCESS TULIP TO MARRY HIM--EVEN THOUGH WE ALL KNOW SHE'S IN LOVE WITH MUCHE-MUCHE.

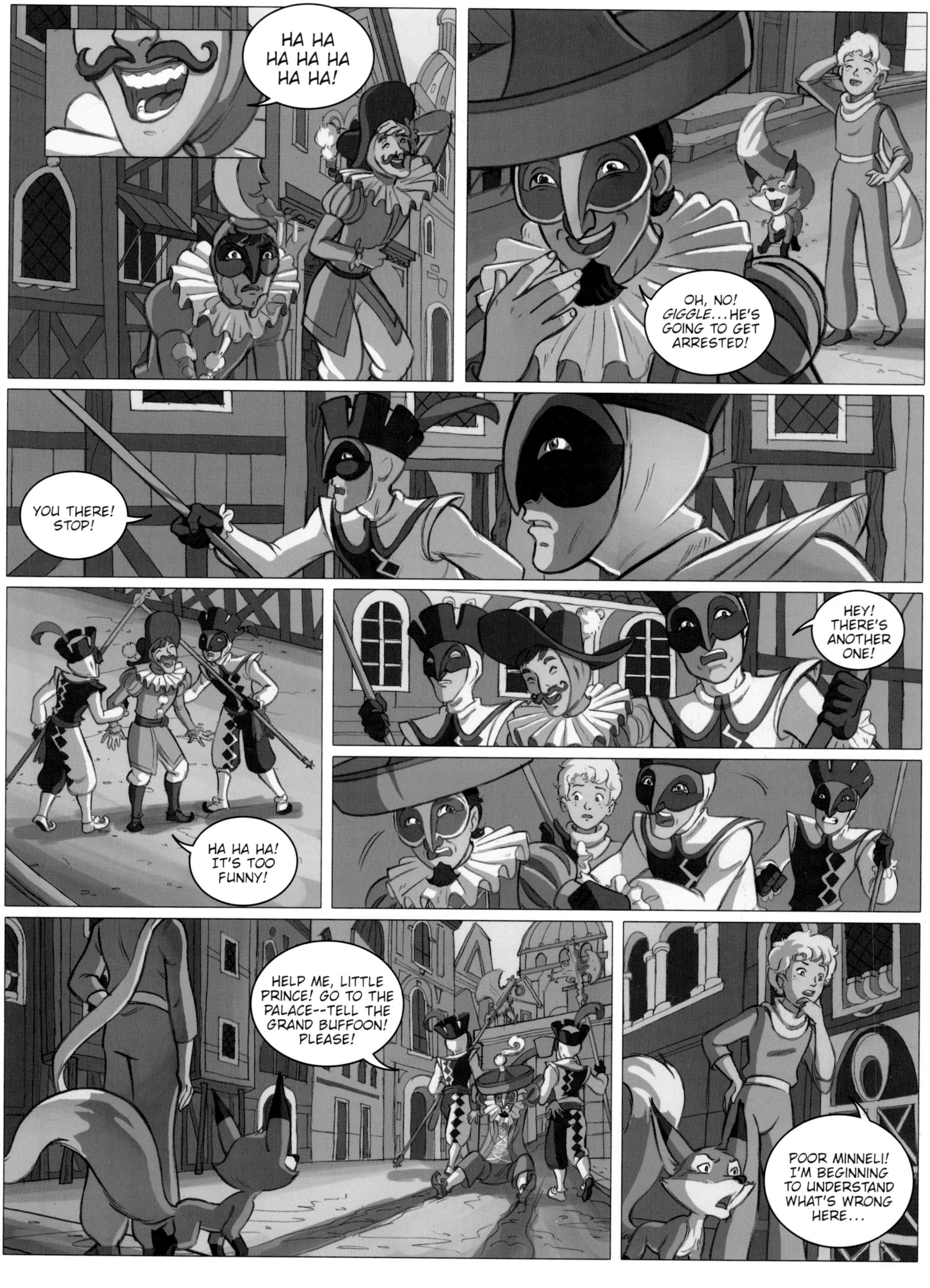
HA HA
HA HA HA
HA HA!
OH, NO! GIGGLE... HE'S GOING TO GET ARRESTED!
YOU THERE! STOP!
HA HA HA! IT'S TOO FUNNY!
HEY! THERE'S ANOTHER ONE!
HELP ME, LITTLE PRINCE! GO TO THE PALACE--TELL THE GRAND BUFFOON! PLEASE!
POOR MINNELI! I'M BEGINNING TO UNDERSTAND WHAT'S WRONG HERE...

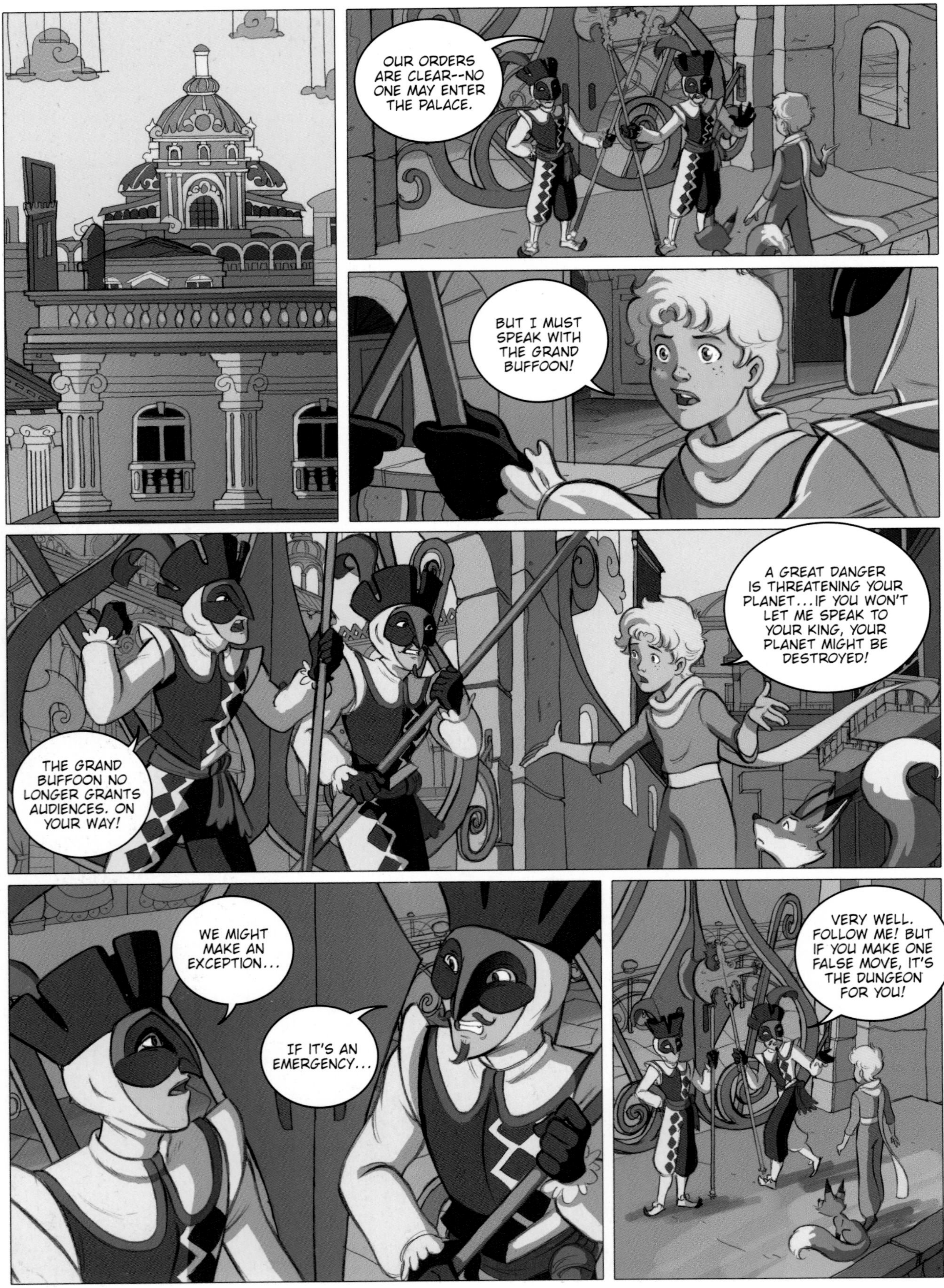
OUR ORDERS ARE CLEAR--NO ONE MAY ENTER THE PALACE.
BUT I MUST SPEAK WITH THE GRAND BUFFOON!
A GREAT DANGER IS THREATENING YOUR PLANET... IF YOU WON'T LET ME SPEAK TO YOUR KING, YOUR PLANET MIGHT BE DESTROYED!
THE GRAND BUFFOON NO LONGER GRANTS AUDIENCES. ON YOUR WAY!
WE MIGHT MAKE AN EXCEPTION...
IF IT'S AN EMERGENCY...
VERY WELL. FOLLOW ME! BUT IF YOU MAKE ONE FALSE MOVE, IT'S THE DUNGEON FOR YOU!

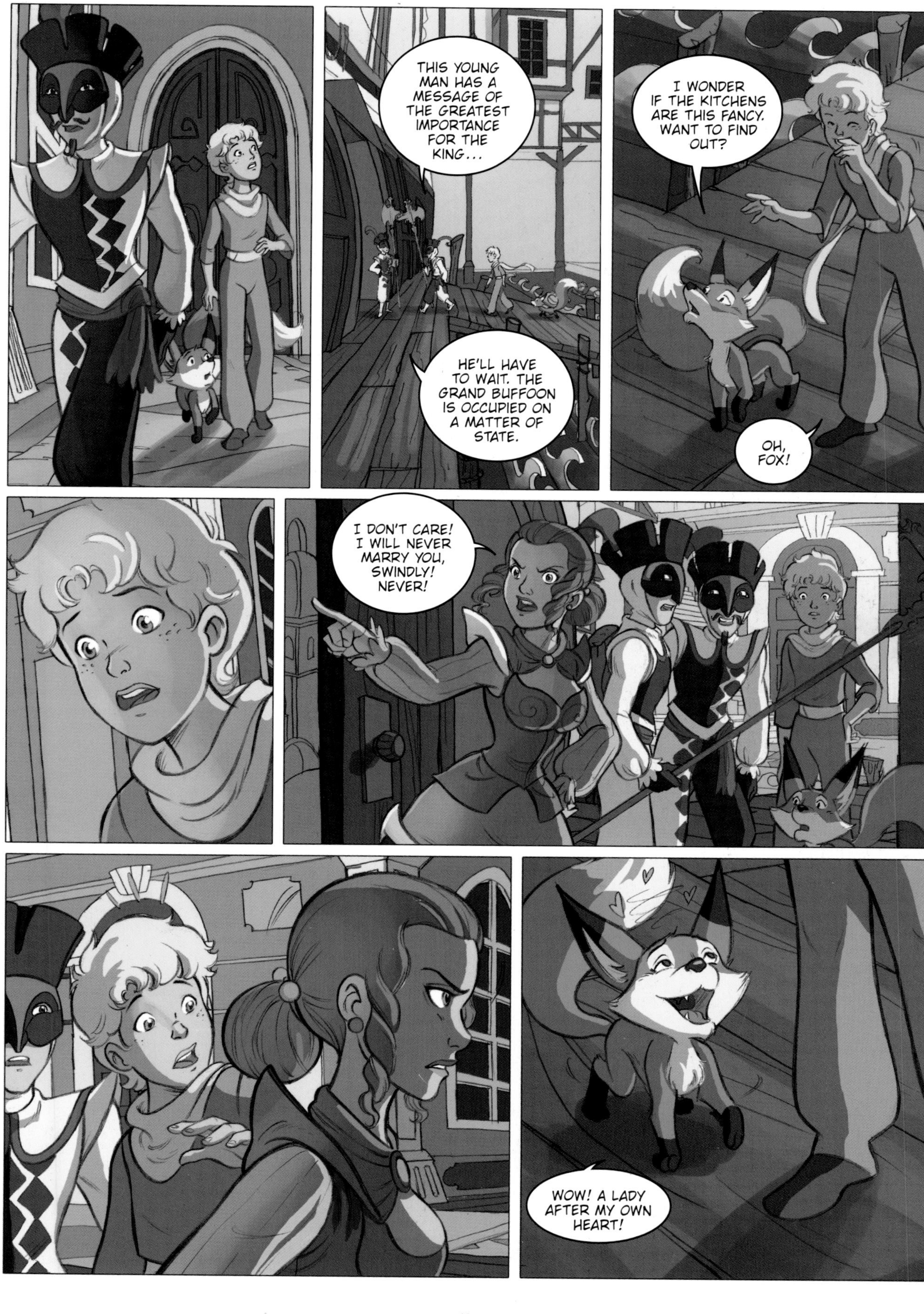
THIS YOUNG MAN HAS A MESSAGE OF THE GREATEST IMPORTANCE FOR THE KING...
HE'LL HAVE TO WAIT. THE GRAND BUFFOON IS OCCUPIED ON A MATTER OF STATE.
I WONDER IF THE KITCHENS ARE THIS FANCY. WANT TO FIND OUT?
OH, FOX!
I DON'T CARE! I WILL NEVER MARRY YOU, SWINDLY! NEVER!
WOW! A LADY AFTER MY OWN HEART!

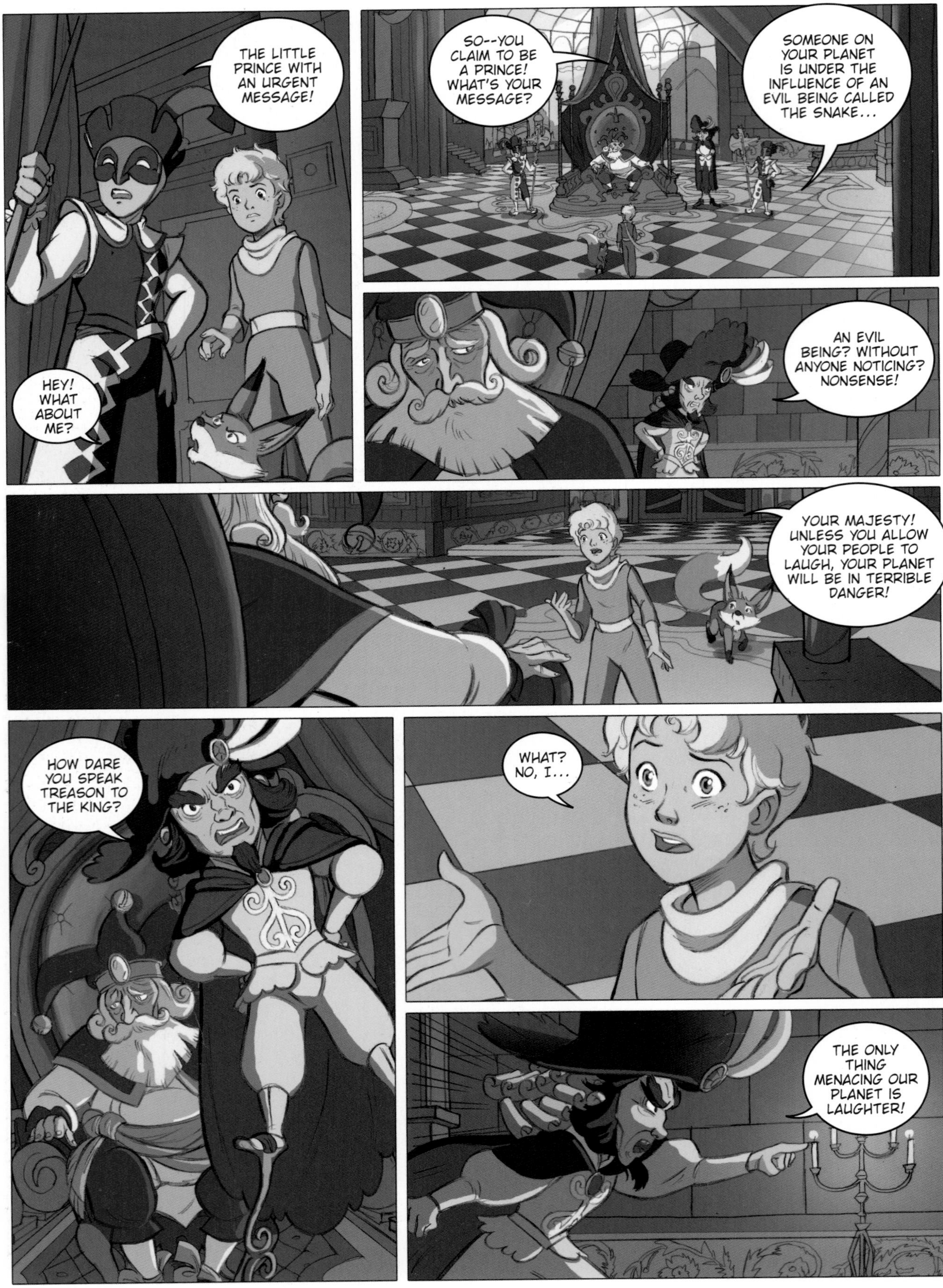
THE LITTLE PRINCE WITH AN URGENT MESSAGE!
HEY! WHAT ABOUT ME?
SO--YOU CLAIM TO BE A PRINCE! WHAT'S YOUR MESSAGE?
SOMEONE ON YOUR PLANET IS UNDER THE INFLUENCE OF AN EVIL BEING CALLED THE SNAKE...
AN EVIL BEING? WITHOUT ANYONE NOTICING? NONSENSE!
YOUR MAJESTY! UNLESS YOU ALLOW YOUR PEOPLE TO LAUGH, YOUR PLANET WILL BE IN TERRIBLE DANGER!
HOW DARE YOU SPEAK TREASON TO THE KING?
WHAT? NO, I...
THE ONLY THING MENACING OUR PLANET IS LAUGHTER!

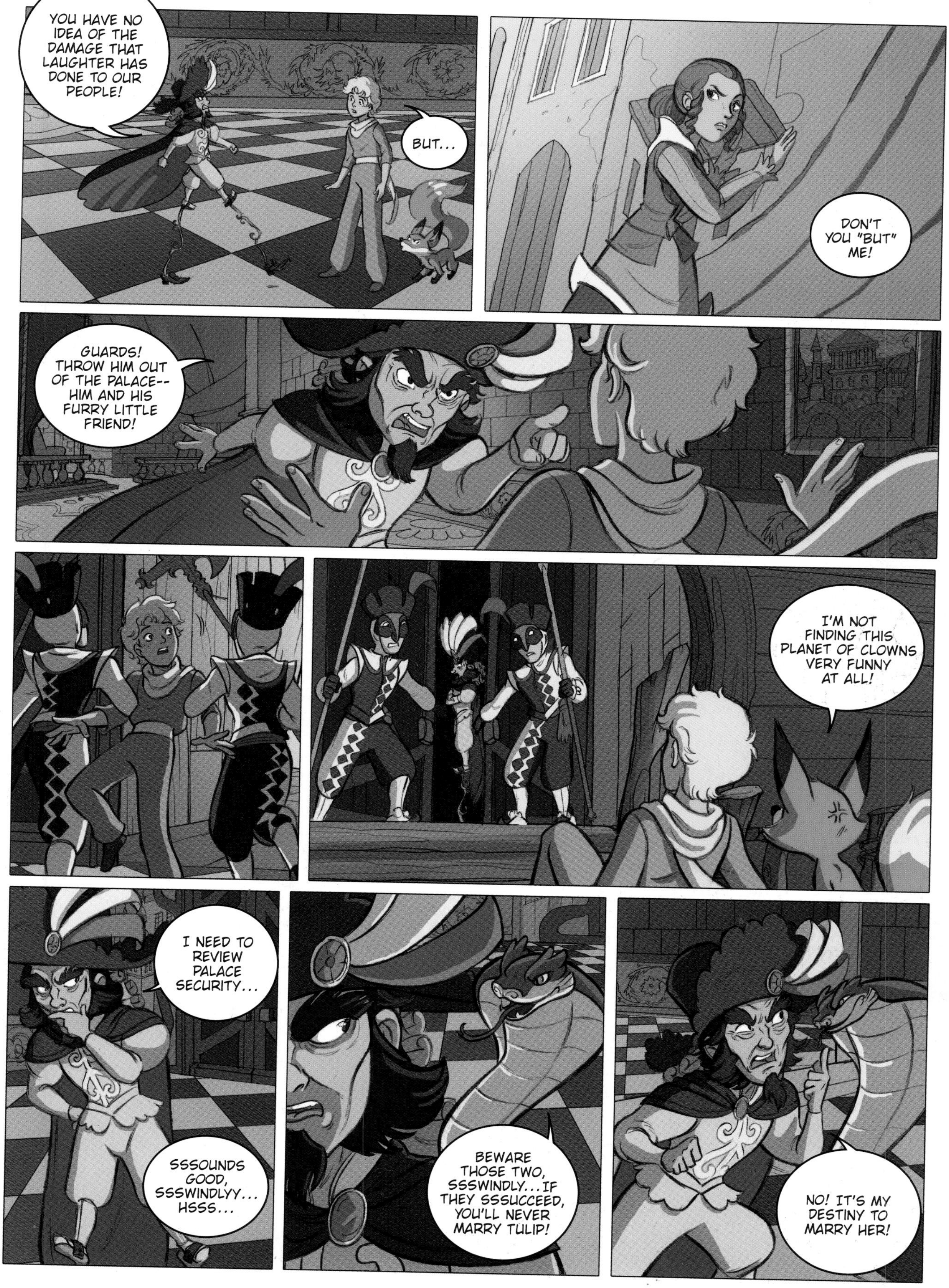
YOU HAVE NO IDEA OF THE DAMAGE THAT LAUGHTER HAS DONE TO OUR PEOPLE!
BUT...
DON'T YOU "BUT" ME!
GUARDS! THROW HIM OUT OF THE PALACE-- HIM AND HIS FURRY LITTLE FRIEND!
I'M NOT FINDING THIS PLANET OF CLOWNS VERY FUNNY AT ALL!
I NEED TO REVIEW PALACE SECURITY...
SSSOUNDS GOOD, SSSWINDLYY... HSSS...
BEWARE THOSE TWO, SSSWINDLY... IF THEY SSSUCCEED, YOU'LL NEVER MARRY TULIP!
NO! IT'S MY DESTINY TO MARRY HER!

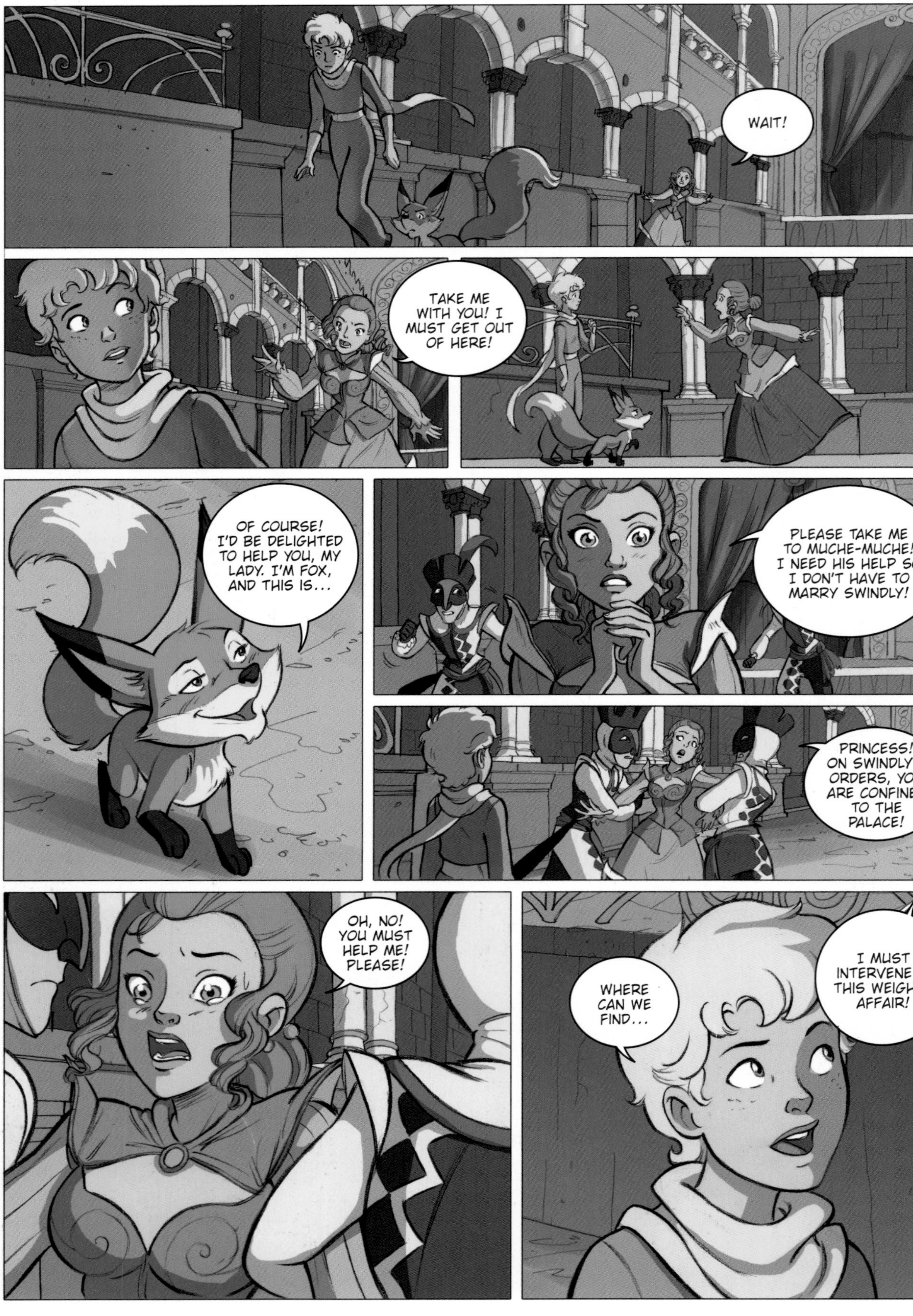
WAIT!
TAKE ME WITH YOU! I MUST GET OUT OF HERE!
OF COURSE! I'D BE DELIGHTED TO HELP YOU, MY LADY. I'M FOX, AND THIS IS...
PLEASE TAKE ME TO MUCHE-MUCHE! I NEED HIS HELP SO I DON'T HAVE TO MARRY SWINDLY!
PRINCESS! ON SWINDLY'S ORDERS, YOU ARE CONFINED TO THE PALACE!
OH, NO! YOU MUST HELP ME! PLEASE!
I MUST INTERVENE IN THIS WEIGHTY AFFAIR!
WHERE CAN WE FIND...

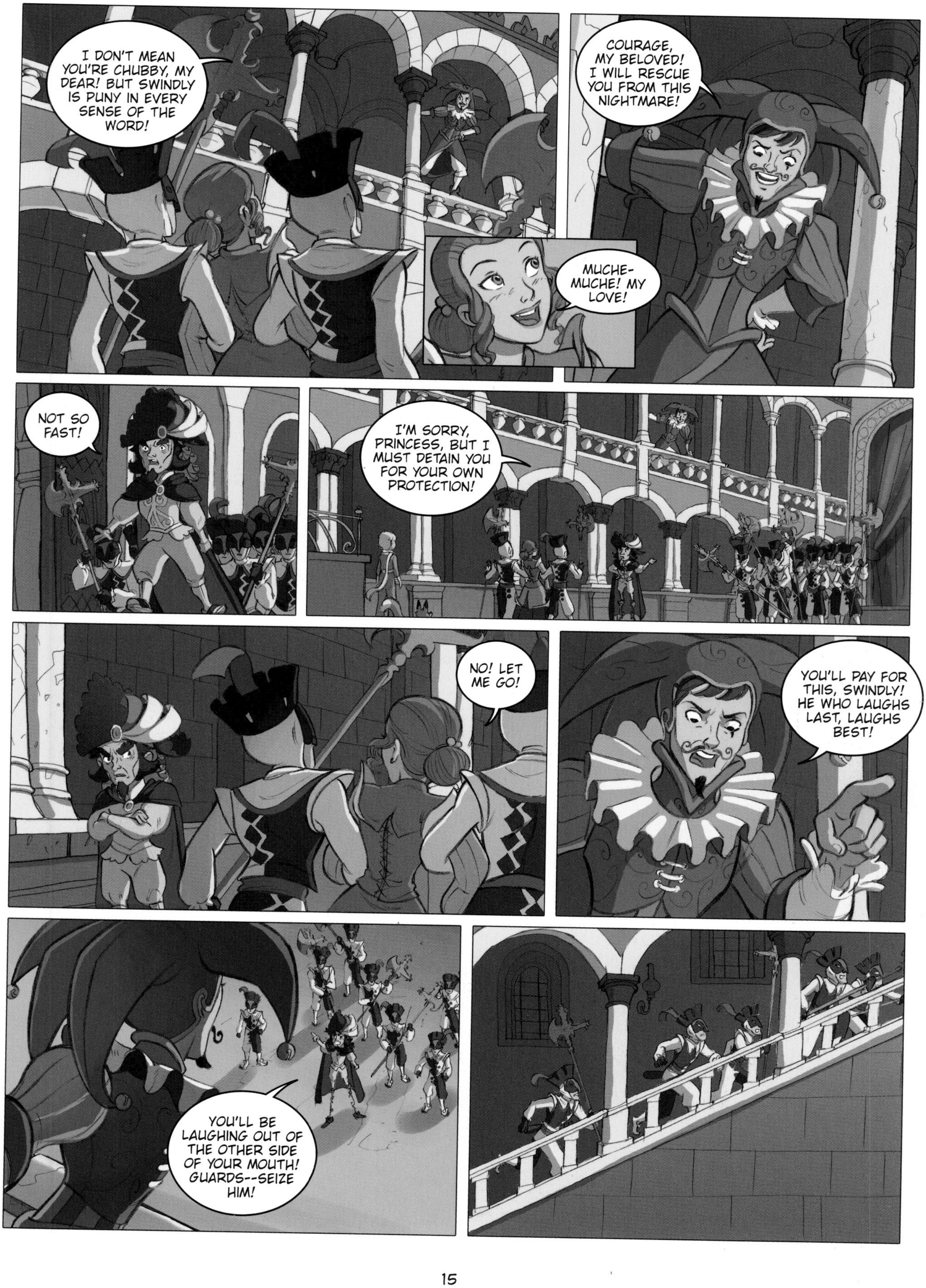
I DON'T MEAN YOU'RE CHUBBY, MY DEAR! BUT SWINDLY IS PUNY IN EVERY SENSE OF THE WORD!
COURAGE, MY BELOVED! I WILL RESCUE YOU FROM THIS NIGHTMARE!
MUCHE-MUCHE! MY LOVE!
NOT SO FAST!
I'M SORRY, PRINCESS, BUT I MUST DETAIN YOU FOR YOUR OWN PROTECTION!
NO! LET ME GO!
YOU'LL PAY FOR THIS, SWINDLY! HE WHO LAUGHS LAST, LAUGHS BEST!
YOU'LL BE LAUGHING OUT OF THE OTHER SIDE OF YOUR MOUTH! GUARDS--SEIZE HIM!

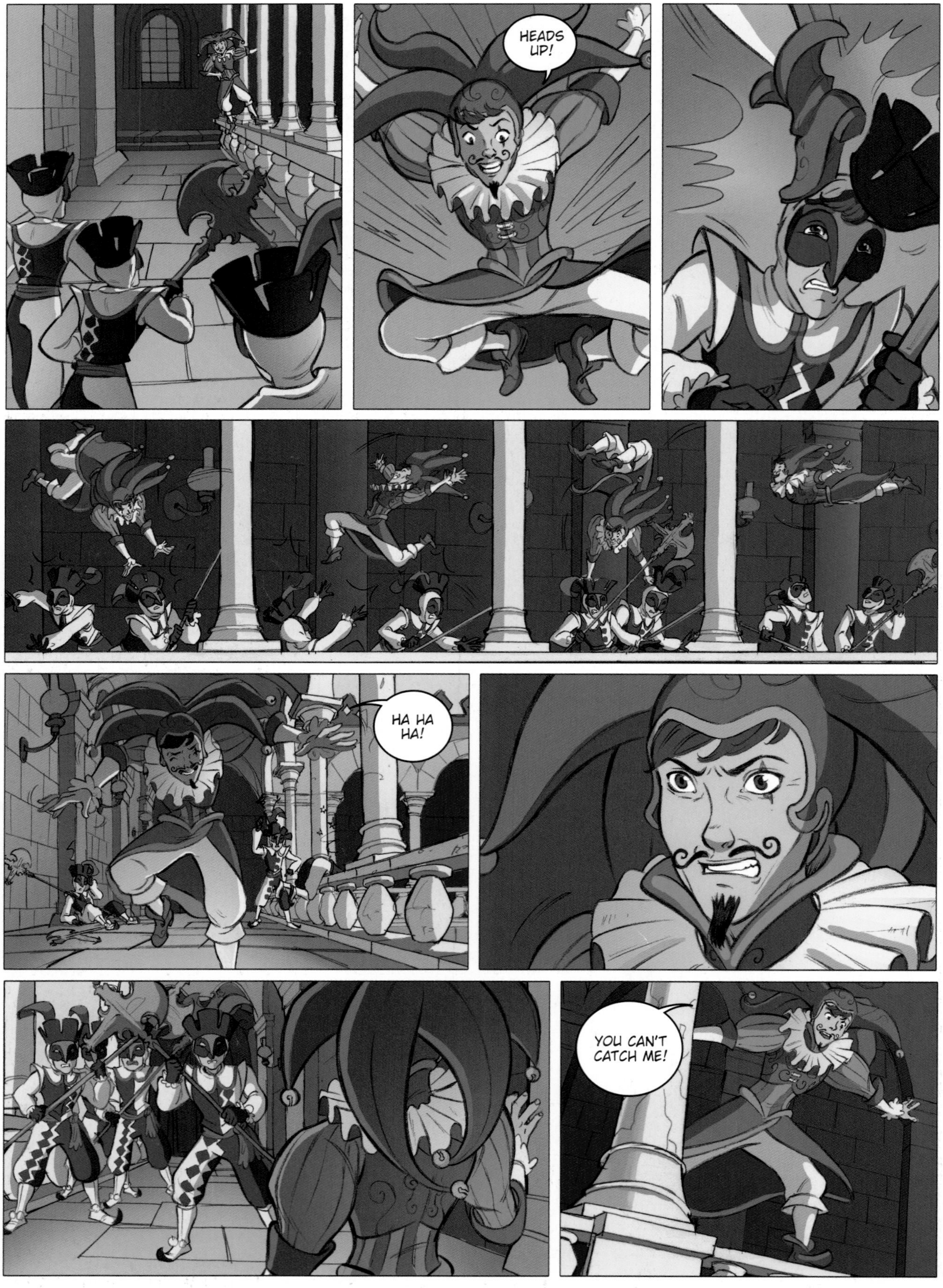
HEADS UP!
HA HA HA!
YOU CAN'T CATCH ME!

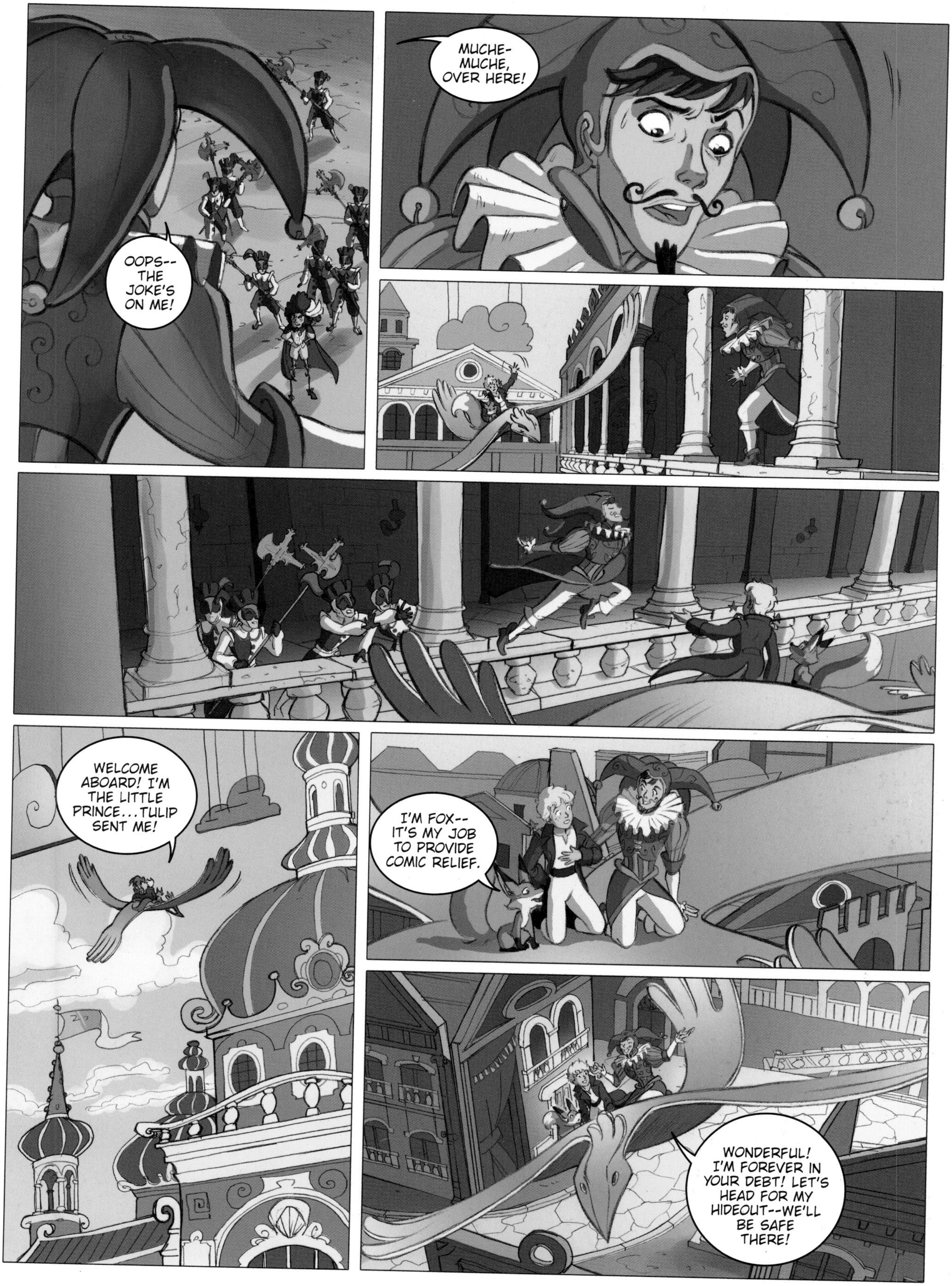
OOPS-- THE JOKE'S ON ME!
MUCHE-MUCHE, OVER HERE!
WELCOME ABOARD! I'M THE LITTLE PRINCE...TULIP SENT ME!
I'M FOX-- IT'S MY JOB TO PROVIDE COMIC RELIEF.
WONDERFUL! I'M FOREVER IN YOUR DEBT! LET'S HEAD FOR MY HIDEOUT--WE'LL BE SAFE THERE!

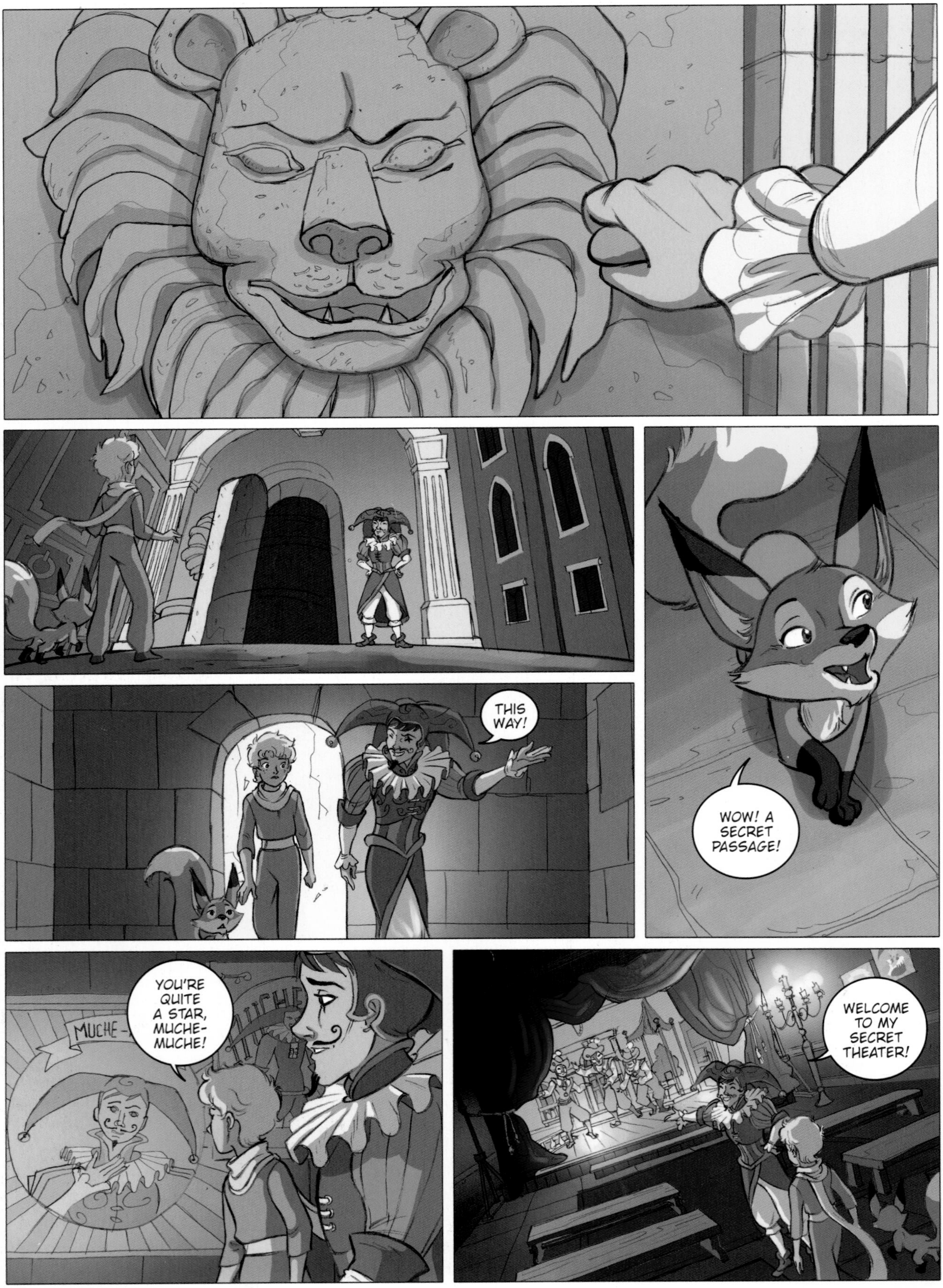
THIS WAY!
WOW! A SECRET PASSAGE!
YOU'RE QUITE A STAR, MUCHE-MUCHE!
WELCOME TO MY SECRET THEATER!

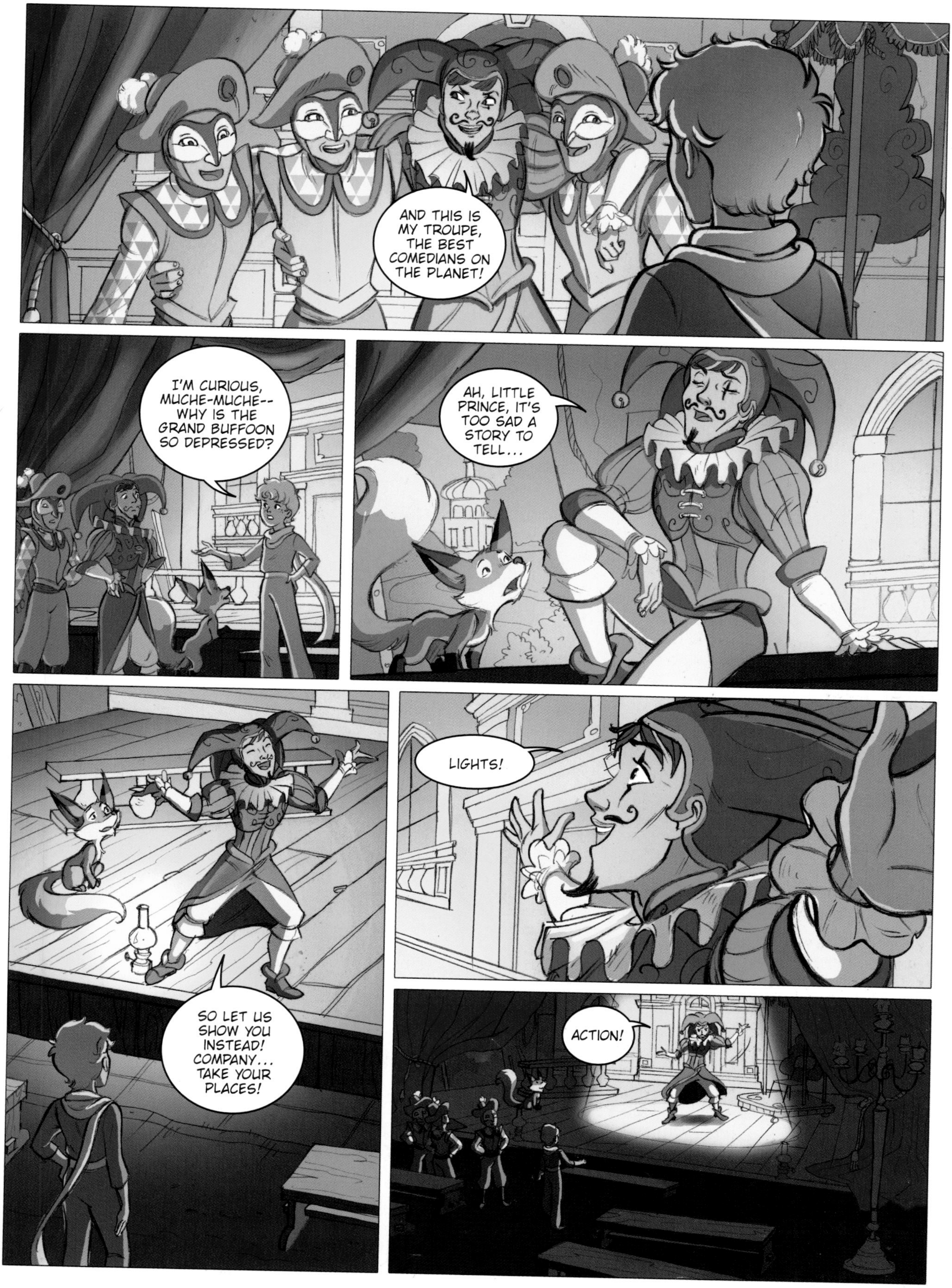
AND THIS IS MY TROUPE, THE BEST COMEDIANS ON THE PLANET!
I'M CURIOUS, MUCHE-MUCHE-- WHY IS THE GRAND BUFFOON SO DEPRESSED?
AH, LITTLE PRINCE, IT'S TOO SAD A STORY TO TELL...
SO LET US SHOW YOU INSTEAD! COMPANY... TAKE YOUR PLACES!
LIGHTS!
ACTION!

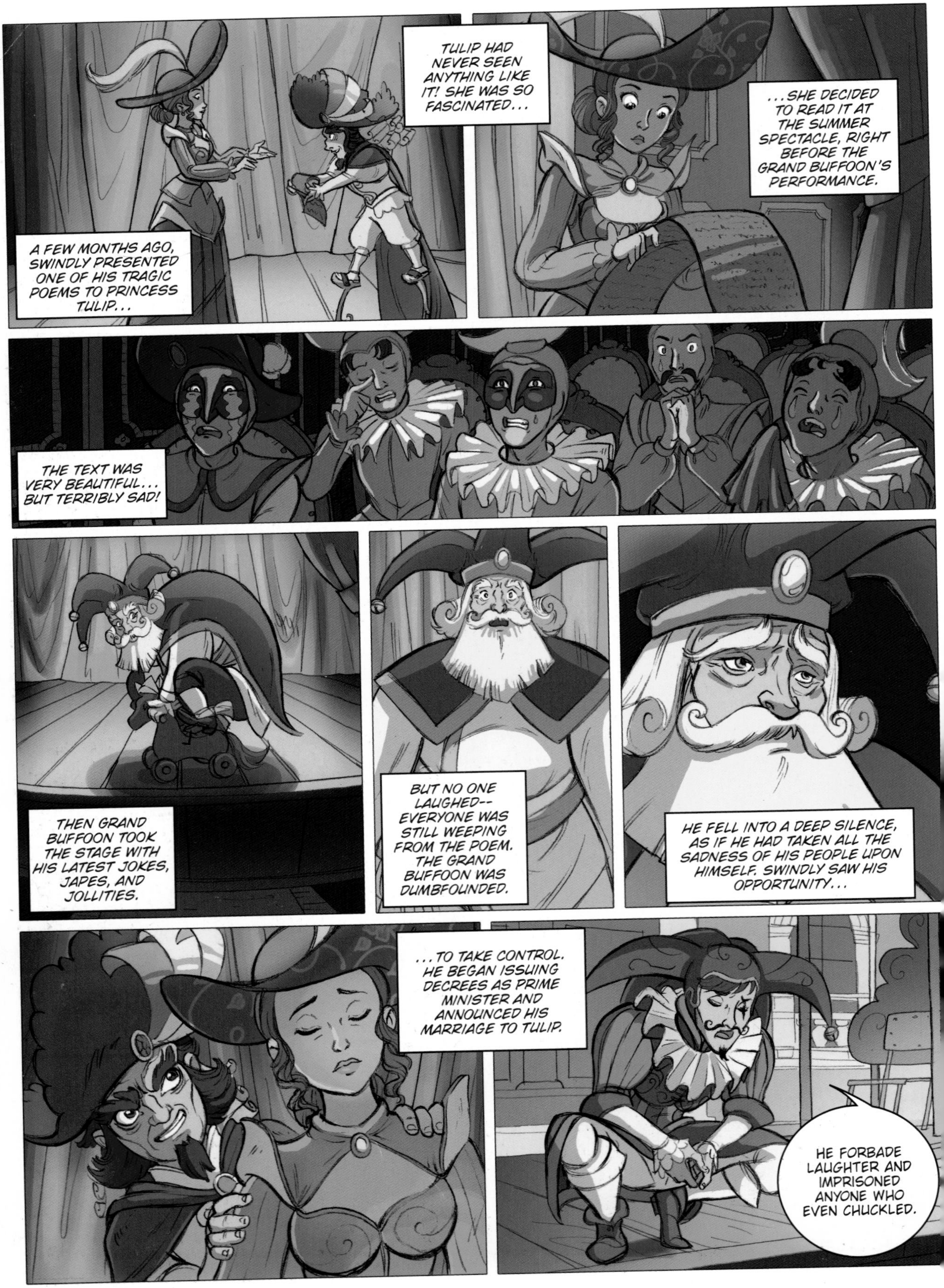
A FEW MONTHS AGO, SWINDLY PRESENTED ONE OF HIS TRAGIC POEMS TO PRINCESS TULIP...
TULIP HAD NEVER SEEN ANYTHING LIKE IT! SHE WAS SO FASCINATED...
...SHE DECIDED TO READ IT AT THE SUMMER SPECTACLE, RIGHT BEFORE THE GRAND BUFFOON'S PERFORMANCE.
THE TEXT WAS VERY BEAUTIFUL... BUT TERRIBLY SAD!
THEN GRAND BUFFOON TOOK THE STAGE WITH HIS LATEST JOKES, JAPES, AND JOLLITIES.
BUT NO ONE LAUGHED--EVERYONE WAS STILL WEEPING FROM THE POEM. THE GRAND BUFFOON WAS DUMBFOUNDED.
HE FELL INTO A DEEP SILENCE, AS IF HE HAD TAKEN ALL THE SADNESS OF HIS PEOPLE UPON HIMSELF. SWINDLY SAW HIS OPPORTUNITY...
...TO TAKE CONTROL. HE BEGAN ISSUING DECREES AS PRIME MINISTER AND ANNOUNCED HIS MARRIAGE TO TULIP.
HE FORBADE LAUGHTER AND IMPRISONED ANYONE WHO EVEN CHUCKLED.

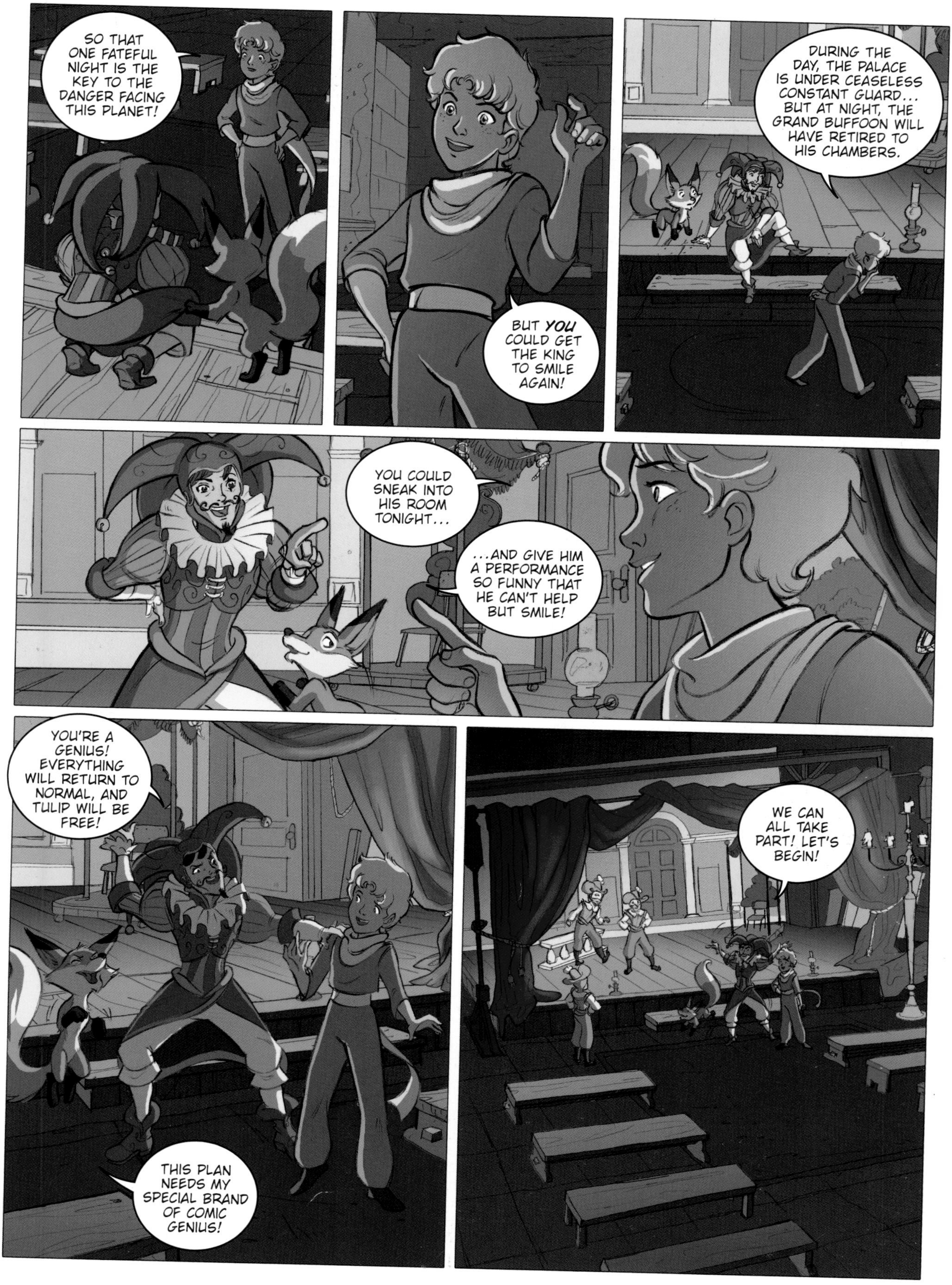
SO THAT ONE FATEFUL NIGHT IS THE KEY TO THE DANGER FACING THIS PLANET!
BUT *YOU* COULD GET THE KING TO SMILE AGAIN!
DURING THE DAY, THE PALACE IS UNDER CEASELESS CONSTANT GUARD... BUT AT NIGHT, THE GRAND BUFFOON WILL HAVE RETIRED TO HIS CHAMBERS.
YOU COULD SNEAK INTO HIS ROOM TONIGHT...
...AND GIVE HIM A PERFORMANCE SO FUNNY THAT HE CAN'T HELP BUT SMILE!
YOU'RE A GENIUS! EVERYTHING WILL RETURN TO NORMAL, AND TULIP WILL BE FREE!
THIS PLAN NEEDS MY SPECIAL BRAND OF COMIC GENIUS!
WE CAN ALL TAKE PART! LET'S BEGIN!

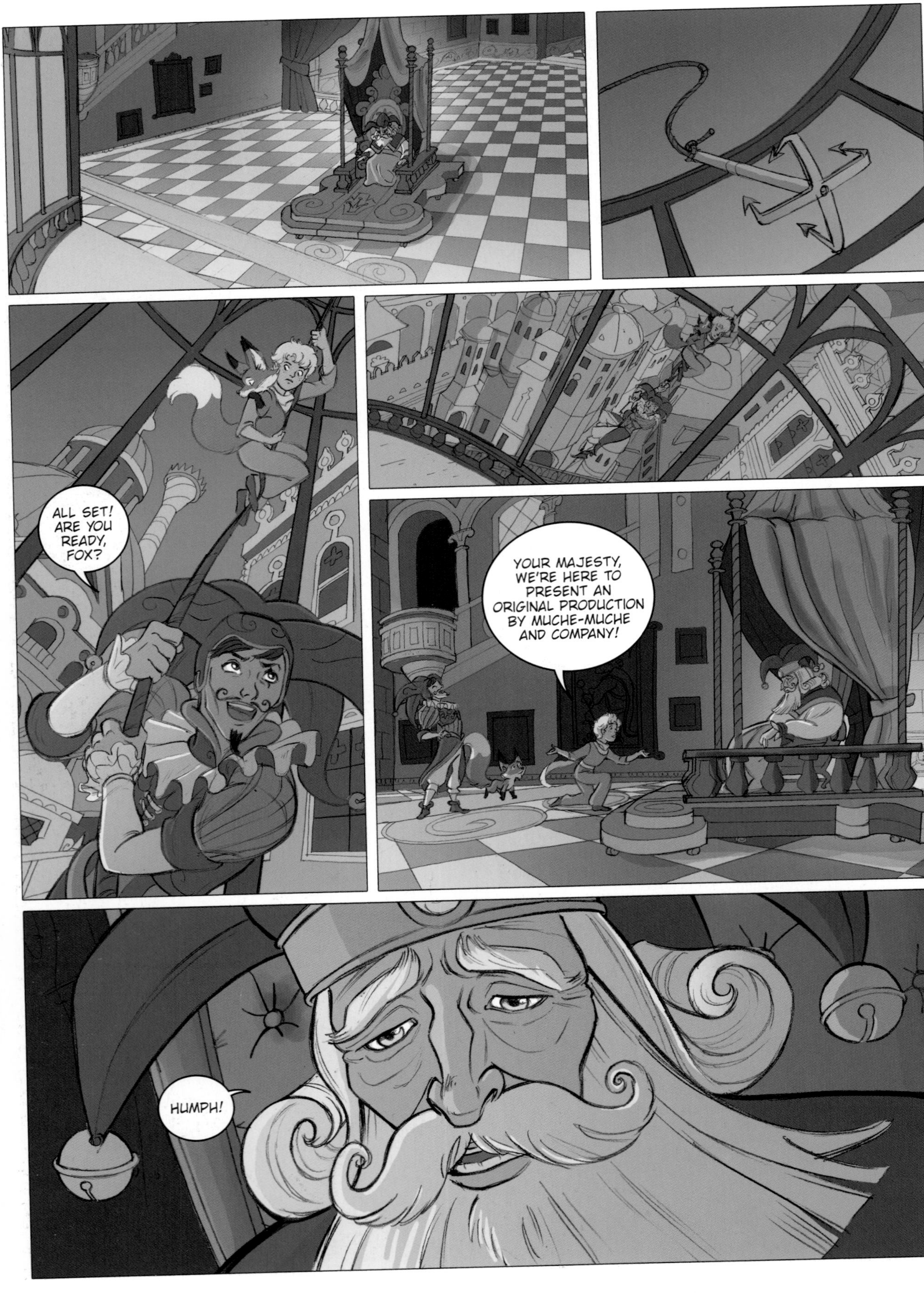
ALL SET! ARE YOU READY, FOX?
YOUR MAJESTY, WE'RE HERE TO PRESENT AN ORIGINAL PRODUCTION BY MUCHE-MUCHE AND COMPANY!
HUMPH!

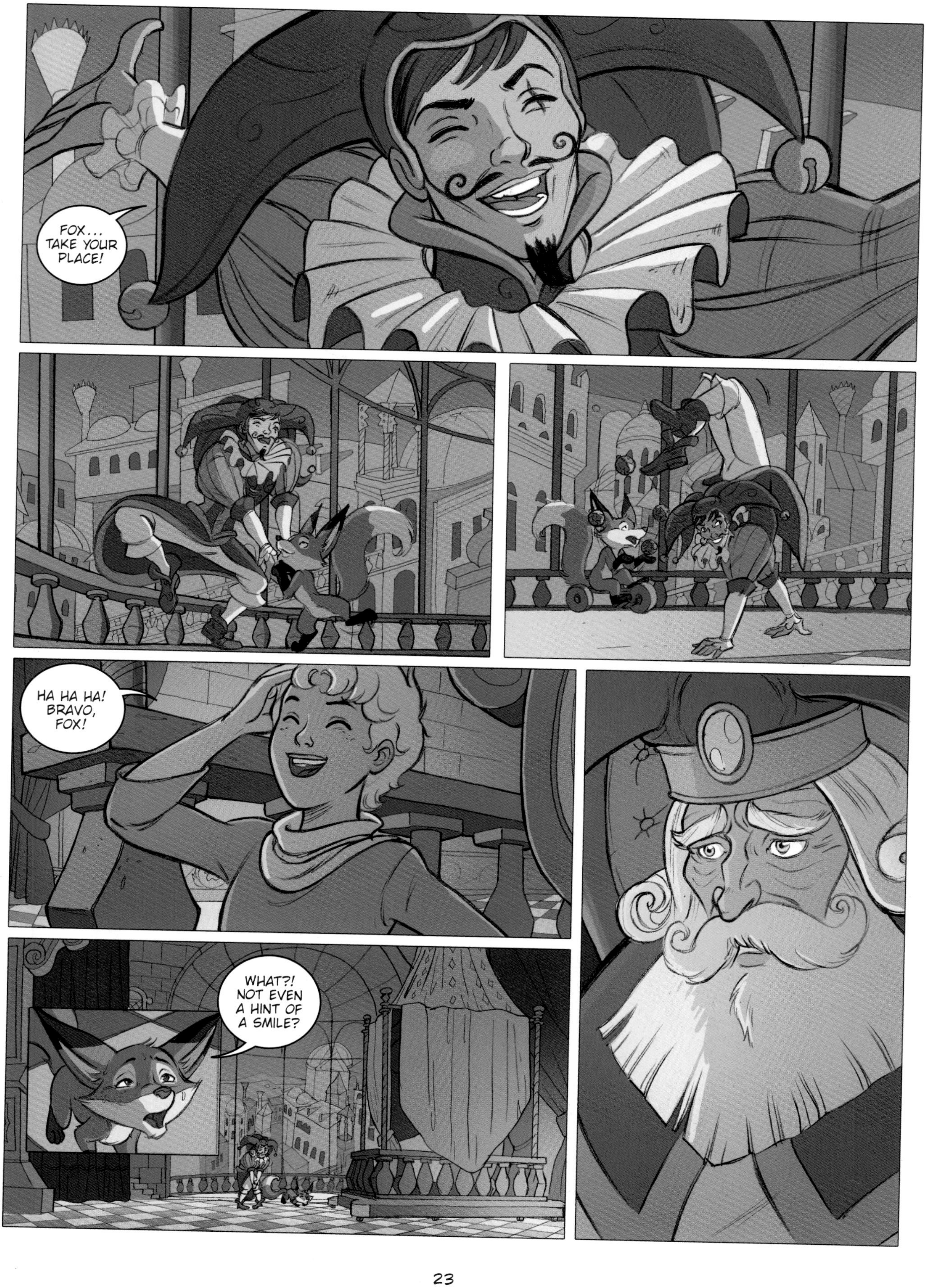
FOX... TAKE YOUR PLACE!
HA HA HA! BRAVO, FOX!
WHAT?! NOT EVEN A HINT OF A SMILE?

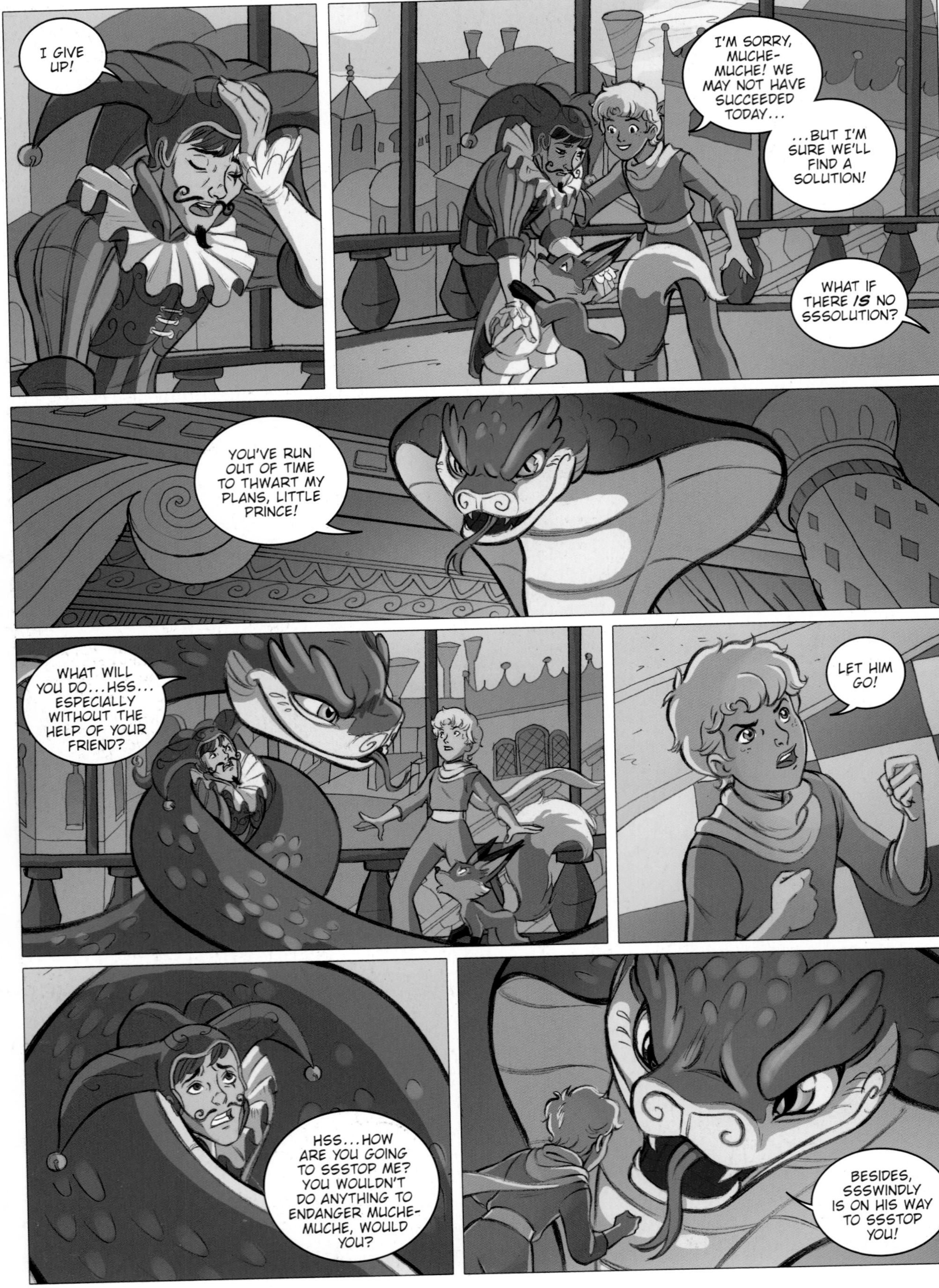
I GIVE UP!
I'M SORRY, MUCHE-MUCHE! WE MAY NOT HAVE SUCCEEDED TODAY...
...BUT I'M SURE WE'LL FIND A SOLUTION!
WHAT IF THERE *IS* NO SSSOLUTION?
YOU'VE RUN OUT OF TIME TO THWART MY PLANS, LITTLE PRINCE!
WHAT WILL YOU DO...HSS... ESPECIALLY WITHOUT THE HELP OF YOUR FRIEND?
LET HIM GO!
HSS...HOW ARE YOU GOING TO SSSTOP ME? YOU WOULDN'T DO ANYTHING TO ENDANGER MUCHE-MUCHE, WOULD YOU?
BESIDES, SSSWINDLY IS ON HIS WAY TO SSSTOP YOU!

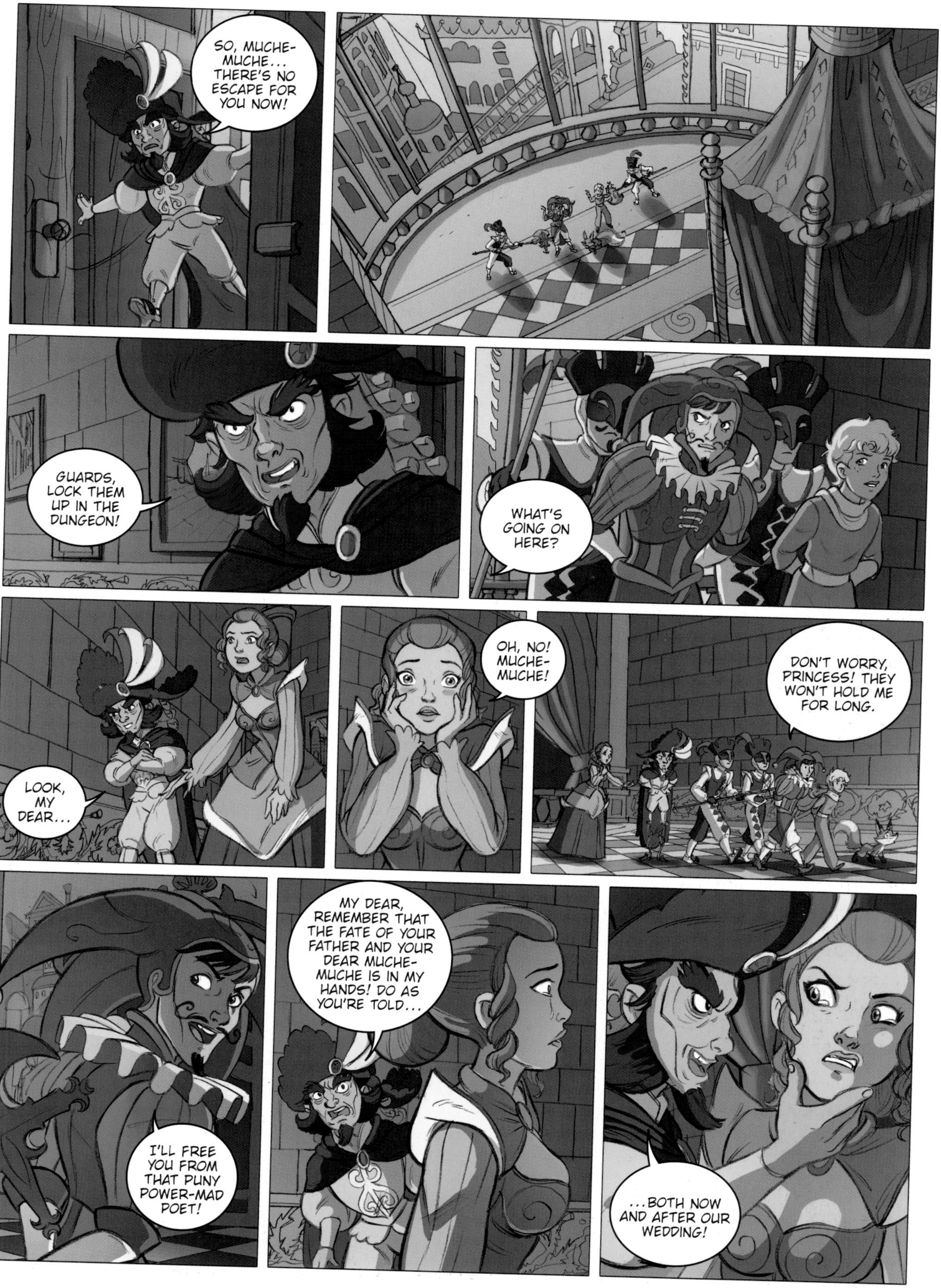
SO, MUCHE-MUCHE... THERE'S NO ESCAPE FOR YOU NOW!
GUARDS, LOCK THEM UP IN THE DUNGEON!
WHAT'S GOING ON HERE?
LOOK, MY DEAR...
OH, NO! MUCHE-MUCHE!
DON'T WORRY, PRINCESS! THEY WON'T HOLD ME FOR LONG.
I'LL FREE YOU FROM THAT PUNY POWER-MAD POET!
MY DEAR, REMEMBER THAT THE FATE OF YOUR FATHER AND YOUR DEAR MUCHE-MUCHE IS IN MY HANDS! DO AS YOU'RE TOLD...
...BOTH NOW AND AFTER OUR WEDDING!

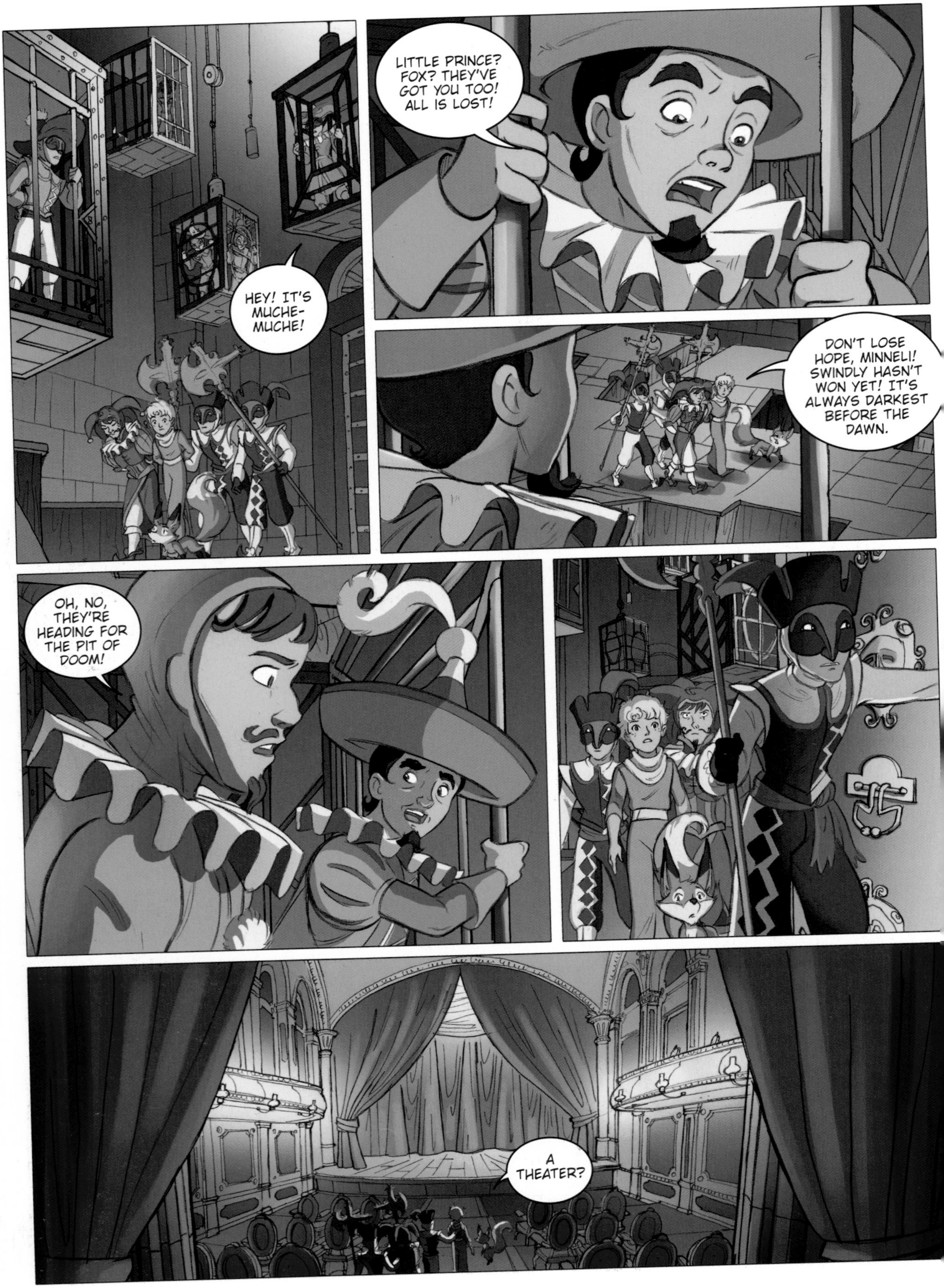
HEY! IT'S MUCHE-MUCHE!
LITTLE PRINCE? FOX? THEY'VE GOT YOU TOO! ALL IS LOST!
DON'T LOSE HOPE, MINNELI! SWINDLY HASN'T WON YET! IT'S ALWAYS DARKEST BEFORE THE DAWN.
OH, NO, THEY'RE HEADING FOR THE PIT OF DOOM!
A THEATER?

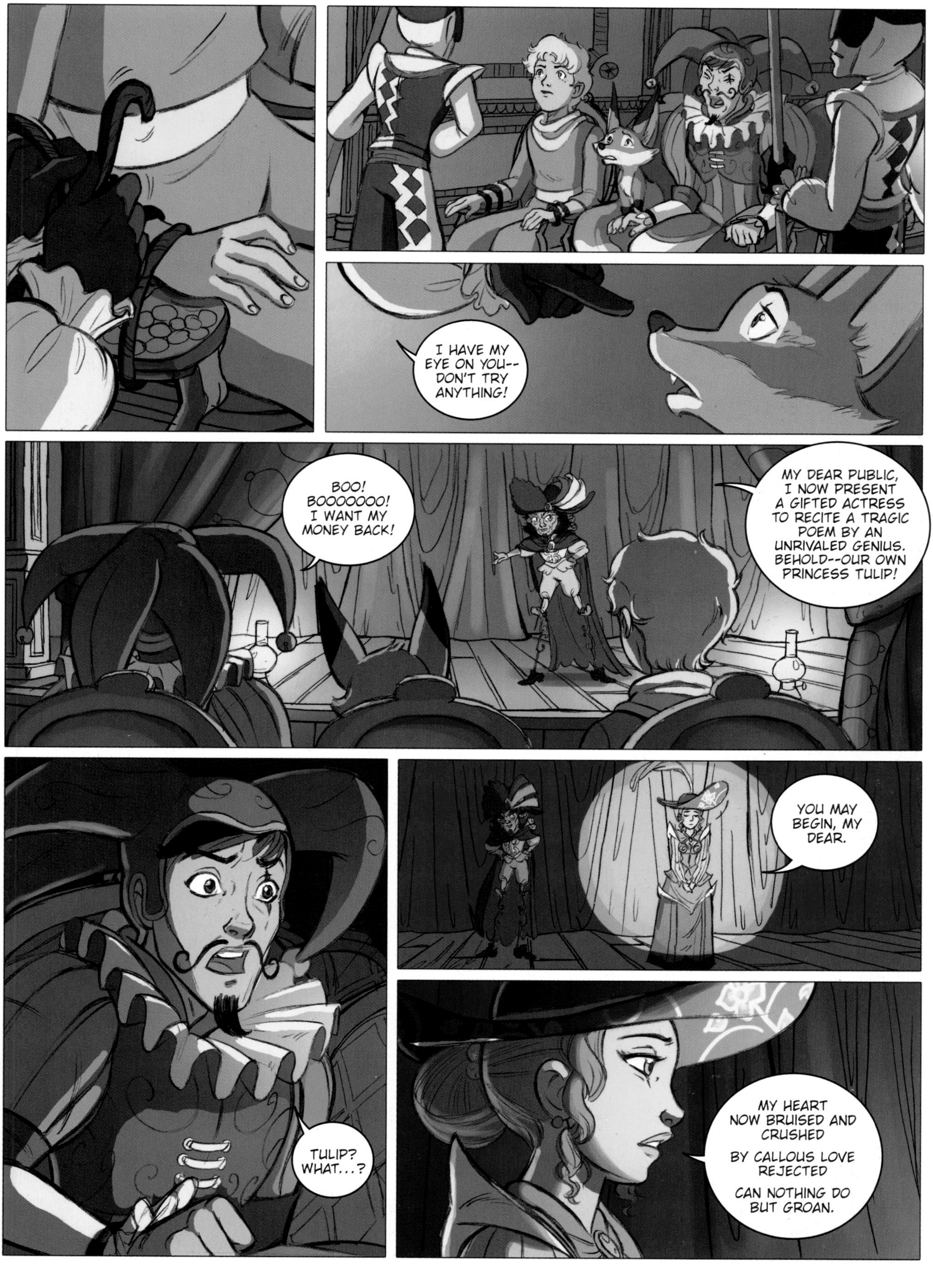

I HAVE MY EYE ON YOU--DON'T TRY ANYTHING!
BOO! BOOOOOOO! I WANT MY MONEY BACK!
MY DEAR PUBLIC, I NOW PRESENT A GIFTED ACTRESS TO RECITE A TRAGIC POEM BY AN UNRIVALED GENIUS. BEHOLD--OUR OWN PRINCESS TULIP!
YOU MAY BEGIN, MY DEAR.
TULIP? WHAT...?
MY HEART NOW BRUISED AND CRUSHED
BY CALLOUS LOVE REJECTED
CAN NOTHING DO BUT GROAN.

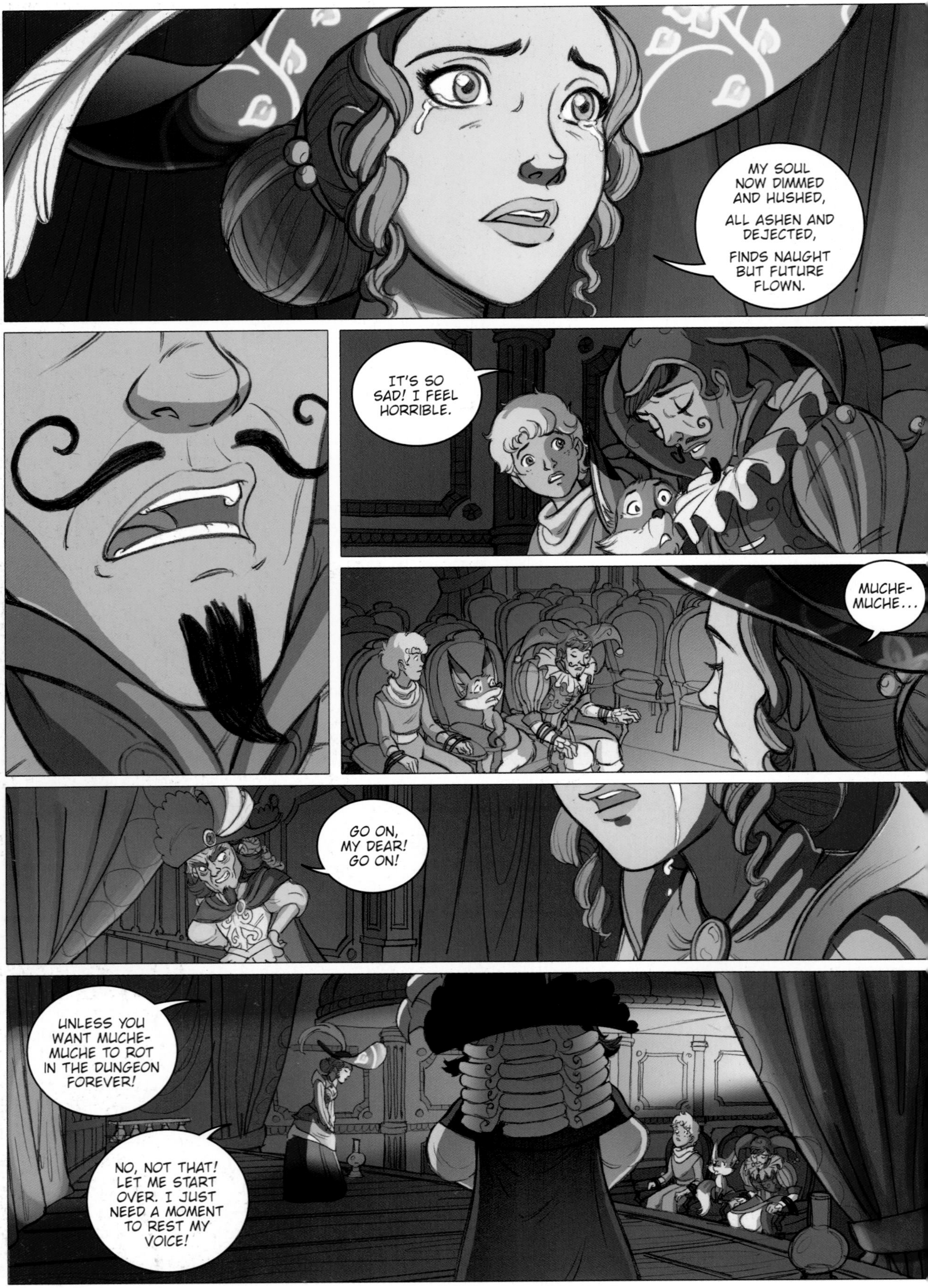
MY SOUL NOW DIMMED AND HUSHED,
ALL ASHEN AND DEJECTED,
FINDS NAUGHT BUT FUTURE FLOWN.
IT'S SO SAD! I FEEL HORRIBLE.
MUCHE-MUCHE...
GO ON, MY DEAR! GO ON!
UNLESS YOU WANT MUCHE-MUCHE TO ROT IN THE DUNGEON FOREVER!
NO, NOT THAT! LET ME START OVER. I JUST NEED A MOMENT TO REST MY VOICE!

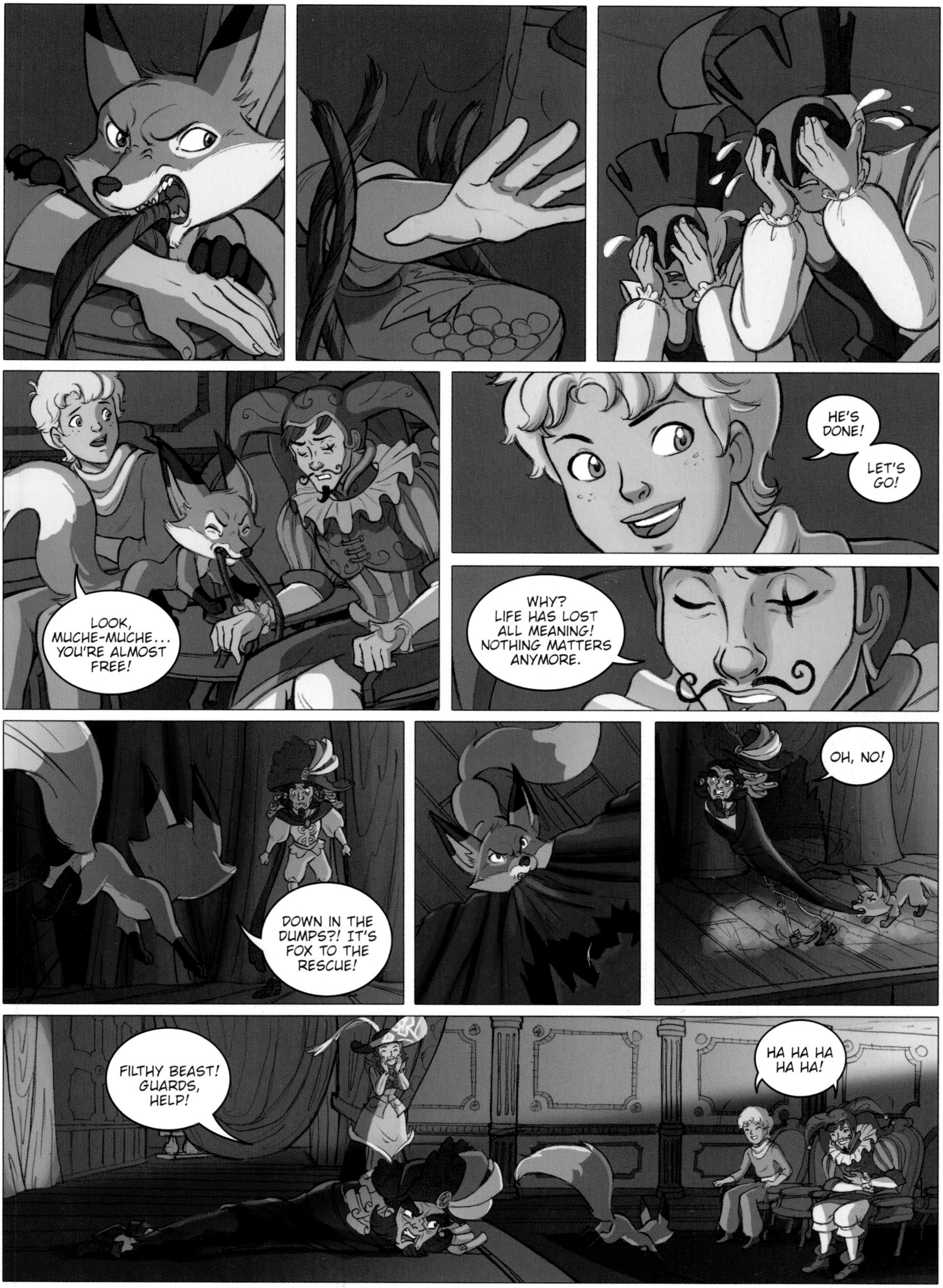
LOOK, MUCHE-MUCHE... YOU'RE ALMOST FREE!
HE'S DONE!
LET'S GO!
WHY? LIFE HAS LOST ALL MEANING! NOTHING MATTERS ANYMORE.
DOWN IN THE DUMPS?! IT'S FOX TO THE RESCUE!
OH, NO!
FILTHY BEAST! GUARDS, HELP!
HA HA HA HA HA!

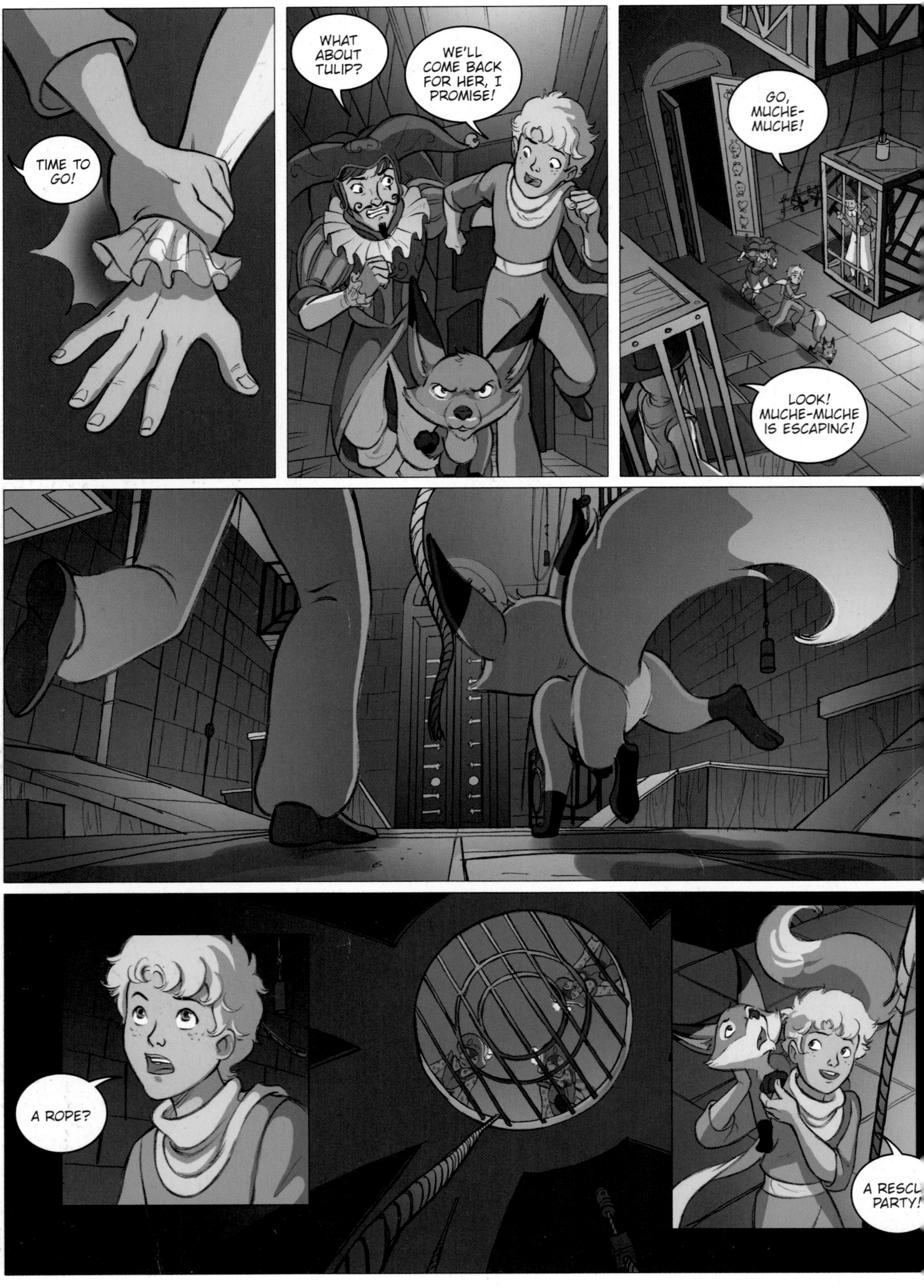
TIME TO GO!
WHAT ABOUT TULIP?
WE'LL COME BACK FOR HER, I PROMISE!
GO, MUCHE-MUCHE!
LOOK! MUCHE-MUCHE IS ESCAPING!
A ROPE?
A RESCU PARTY!

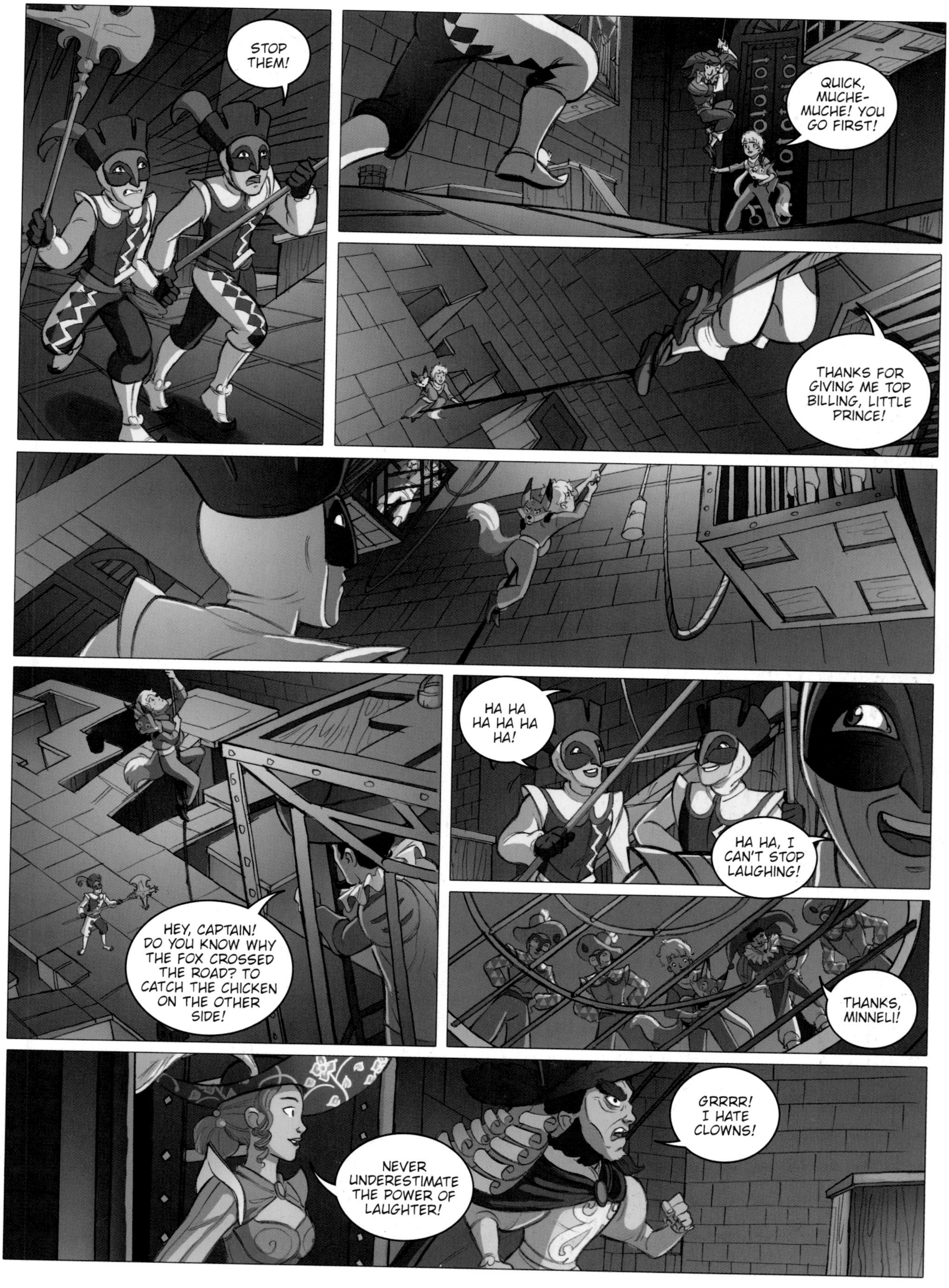
STOP THEM!
QUICK, MUCHE-MUCHE! YOU GO FIRST!
THANKS FOR GIVING ME TOP BILLING, LITTLE PRINCE!
HEY, CAPTAIN! DO YOU KNOW WHY THE FOX CROSSED THE ROAD? TO CATCH THE CHICKEN ON THE OTHER SIDE!
HA HA HA HA HA HA!
HA HA, I CAN'T STOP LAUGHING!
THANKS, MINNELI!
GRRRR! I HATE CLOWNS!
NEVER UNDERESTIMATE THE POWER OF LAUGHTER!

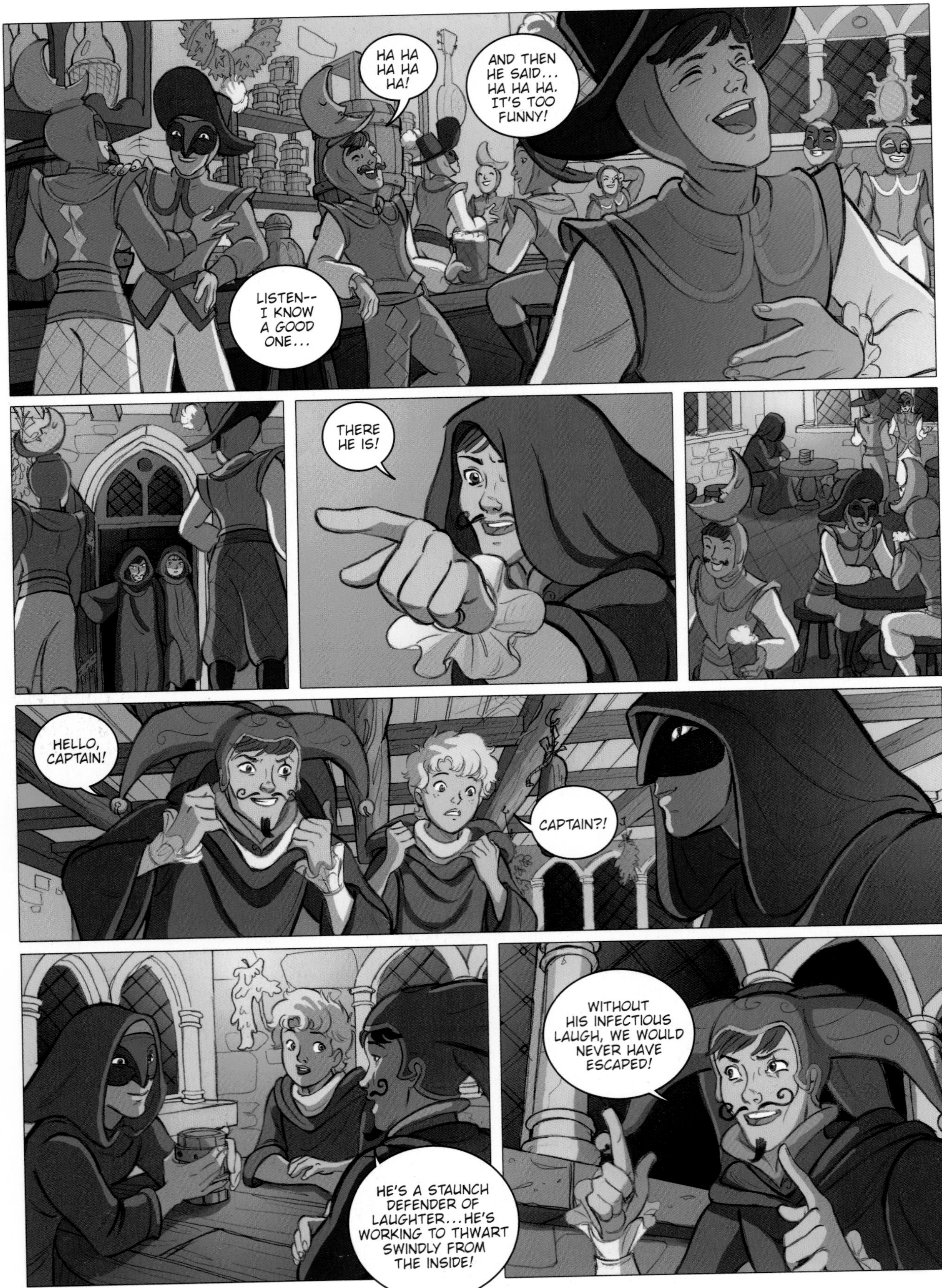
HA HA HA HA HA!
AND THEN HE SAID... HA HA HA. IT'S TOO FUNNY!
LISTEN-- I KNOW A GOOD ONE...
THERE HE IS!
HELLO, CAPTAIN!
CAPTAIN?!
HE'S A STAUNCH DEFENDER OF LAUGHTER... HE'S WORKING TO THWART SWINDLY FROM THE INSIDE!
WITHOUT HIS INFECTIOUS LAUGH, WE WOULD NEVER HAVE ESCAPED!

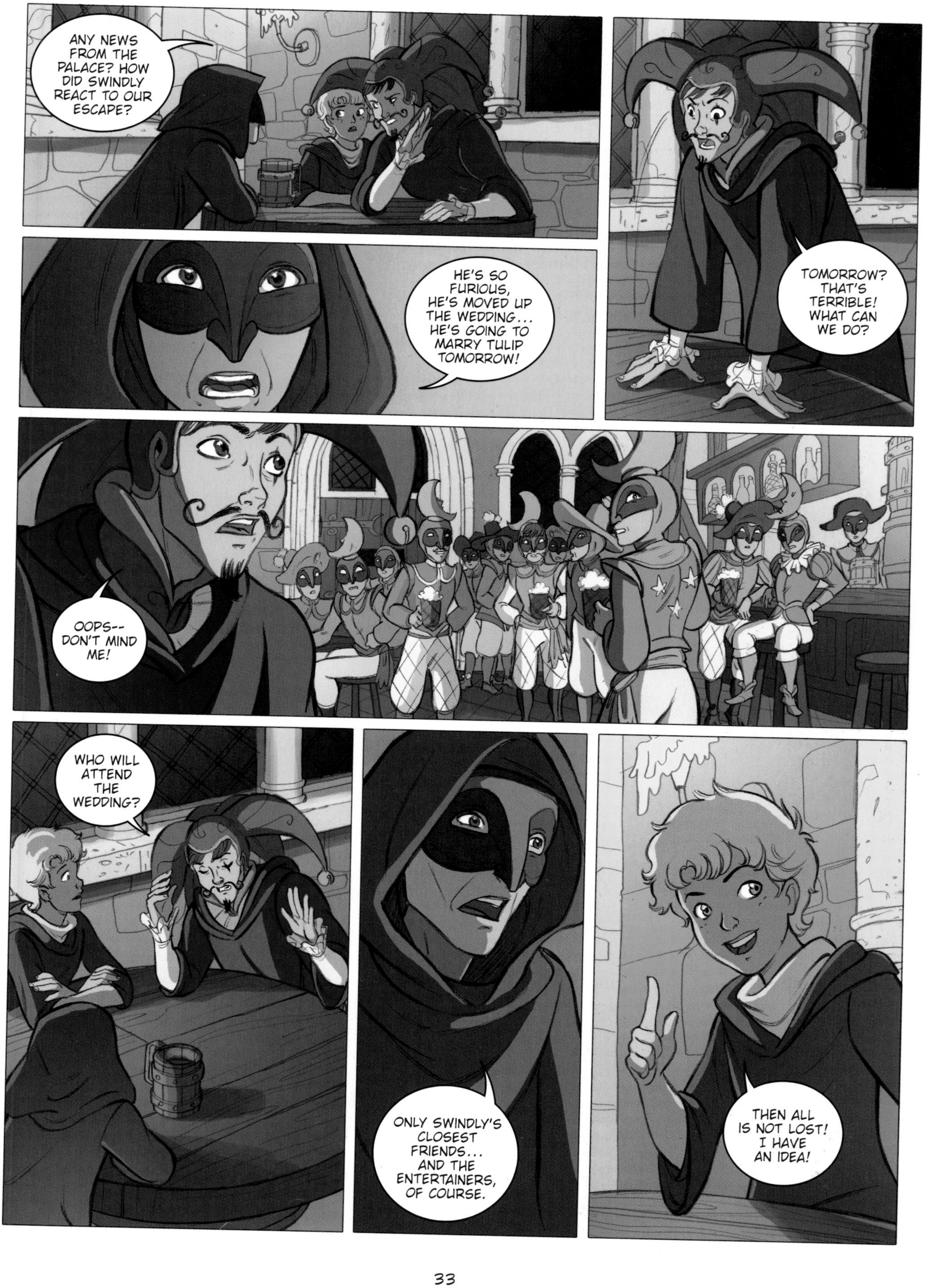
ANY NEWS FROM THE PALACE? HOW DID SWINDLY REACT TO OUR ESCAPE?
HE'S SO FURIOUS, HE'S MOVED UP THE WEDDING... HE'S GOING TO MARRY TULIP TOMORROW!
TOMORROW? THAT'S TERRIBLE! WHAT CAN WE DO?
OOPS-- DON'T MIND ME!
WHO WILL ATTEND THE WEDDING?
ONLY SWINDLY'S CLOSEST FRIENDS... AND THE ENTERTAINERS, OF COURSE.
THEN ALL IS NOT LOST! I HAVE AN IDEA!

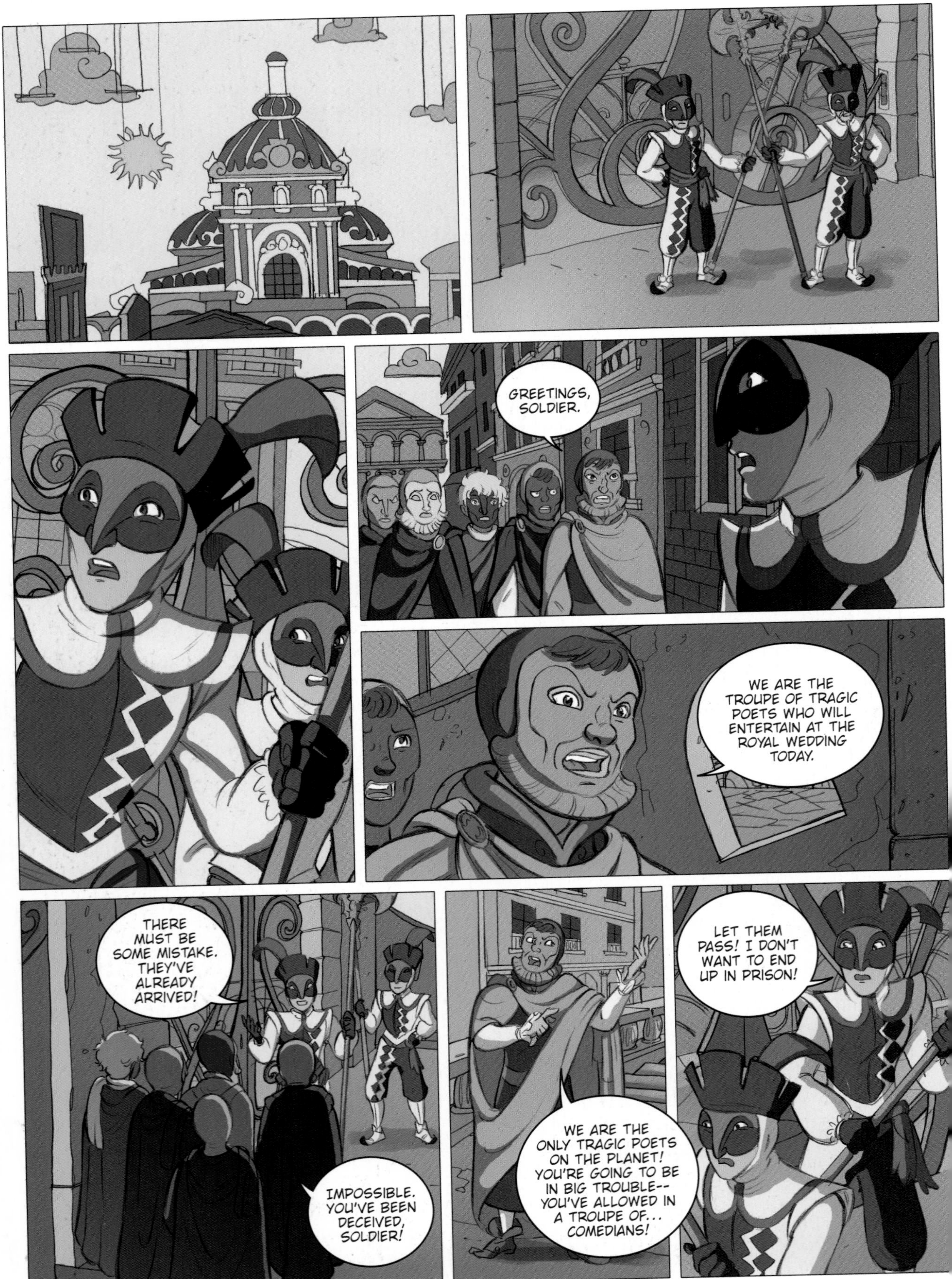
GREETINGS, SOLDIER.
WE ARE THE TROUPE OF TRAGIC POETS WHO WILL ENTERTAIN AT THE ROYAL WEDDING TODAY.
THERE MUST BE SOME MISTAKE. THEY'VE ALREADY ARRIVED!
IMPOSSIBLE. YOU'VE BEEN DECEIVED, SOLDIER!
WE ARE THE ONLY TRAGIC POETS ON THE PLANET! YOU'RE GOING TO BE IN BIG TROUBLE-- YOU'VE ALLOWED IN A TROUPE OF... COMEDIANS!
LET THEM PASS! I DON'T WANT TO END UP IN PRISON!

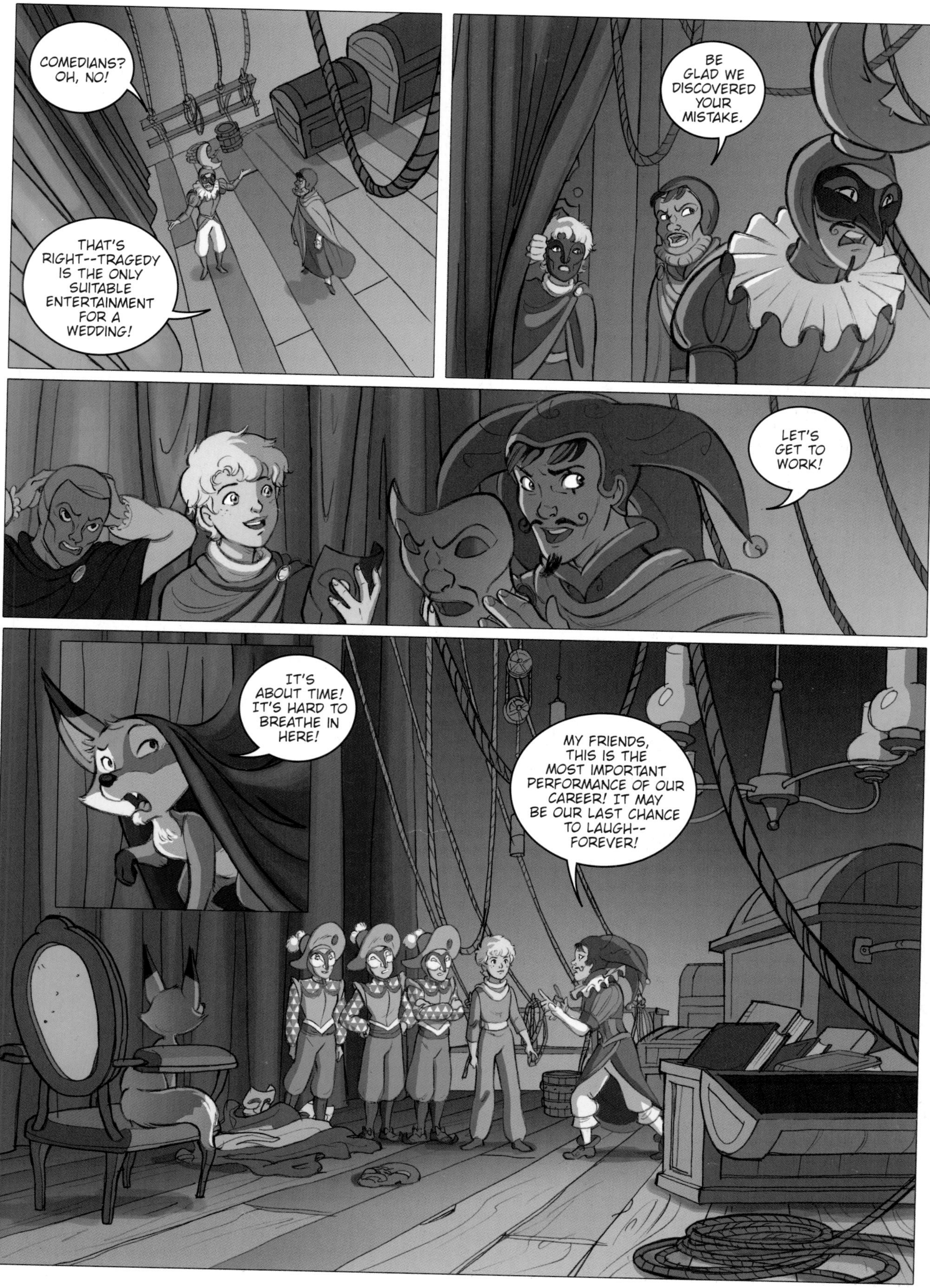
COMEDIANS? OH, NO!
THAT'S RIGHT--TRAGEDY IS THE ONLY SUITABLE ENTERTAINMENT FOR A WEDDING!
BE GLAD WE DISCOVERED YOUR MISTAKE.
LET'S GET TO WORK!
IT'S ABOUT TIME! IT'S HARD TO BREATHE IN HERE!
MY FRIENDS, THIS IS THE MOST IMPORTANT PERFORMANCE OF OUR CAREER! IT MAY BE OUR LAST CHANCE TO LAUGH--FOREVER!

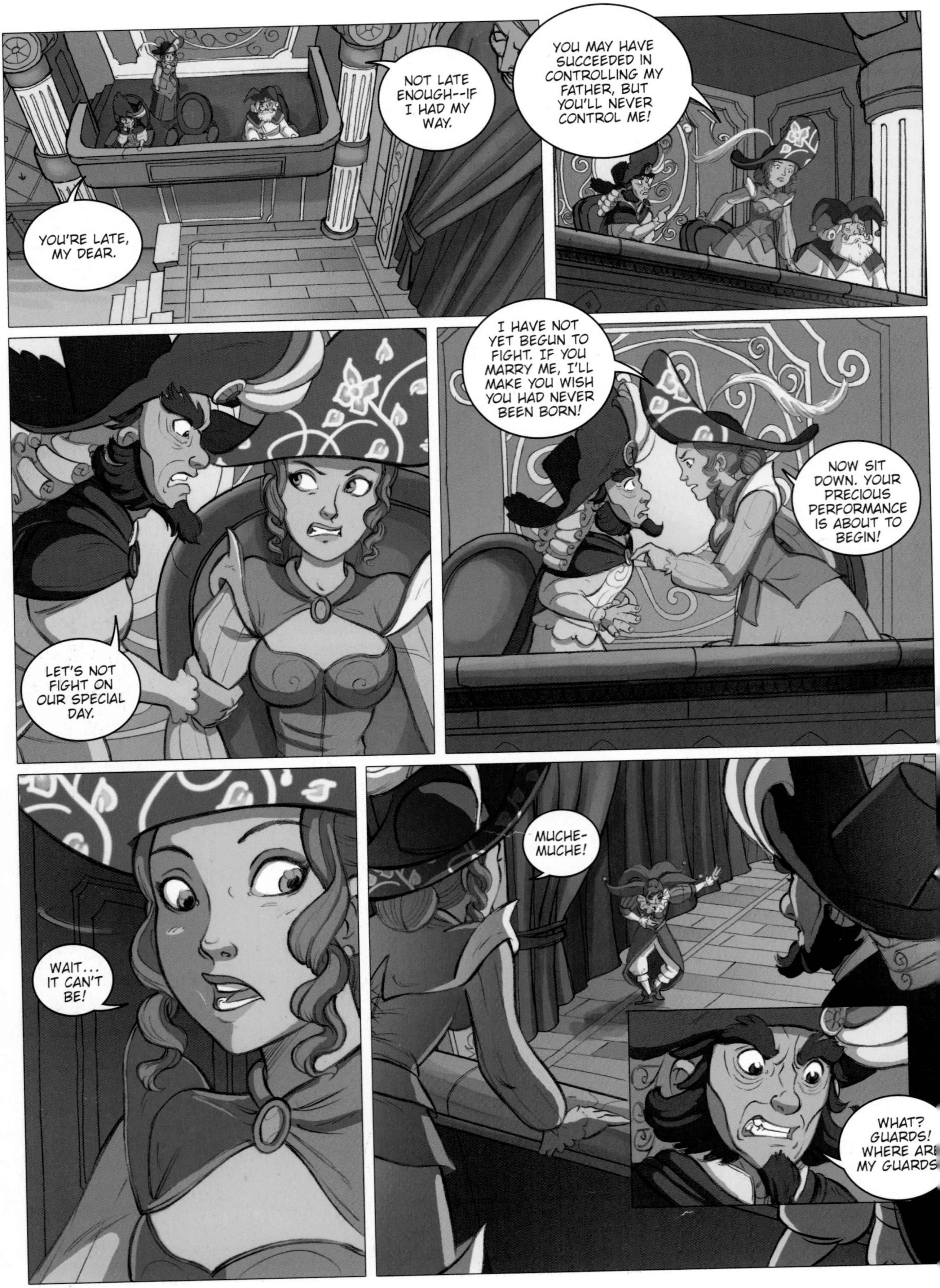
YOU'RE LATE, MY DEAR.
NOT LATE ENOUGH--IF I HAD MY WAY.
YOU MAY HAVE SUCCEEDED IN CONTROLLING MY FATHER, BUT YOU'LL NEVER CONTROL ME!
LET'S NOT FIGHT ON OUR SPECIAL DAY.
I HAVE NOT YET BEGUN TO FIGHT. IF YOU MARRY ME, I'LL MAKE YOU WISH YOU HAD NEVER BEEN BORN!
NOW SIT DOWN. YOUR PRECIOUS PERFORMANCE IS ABOUT TO BEGIN!
WAIT... IT CAN'T BE!
MUCHE-MUCHE!
WHAT? GUARDS! WHERE ARE MY GUARDS

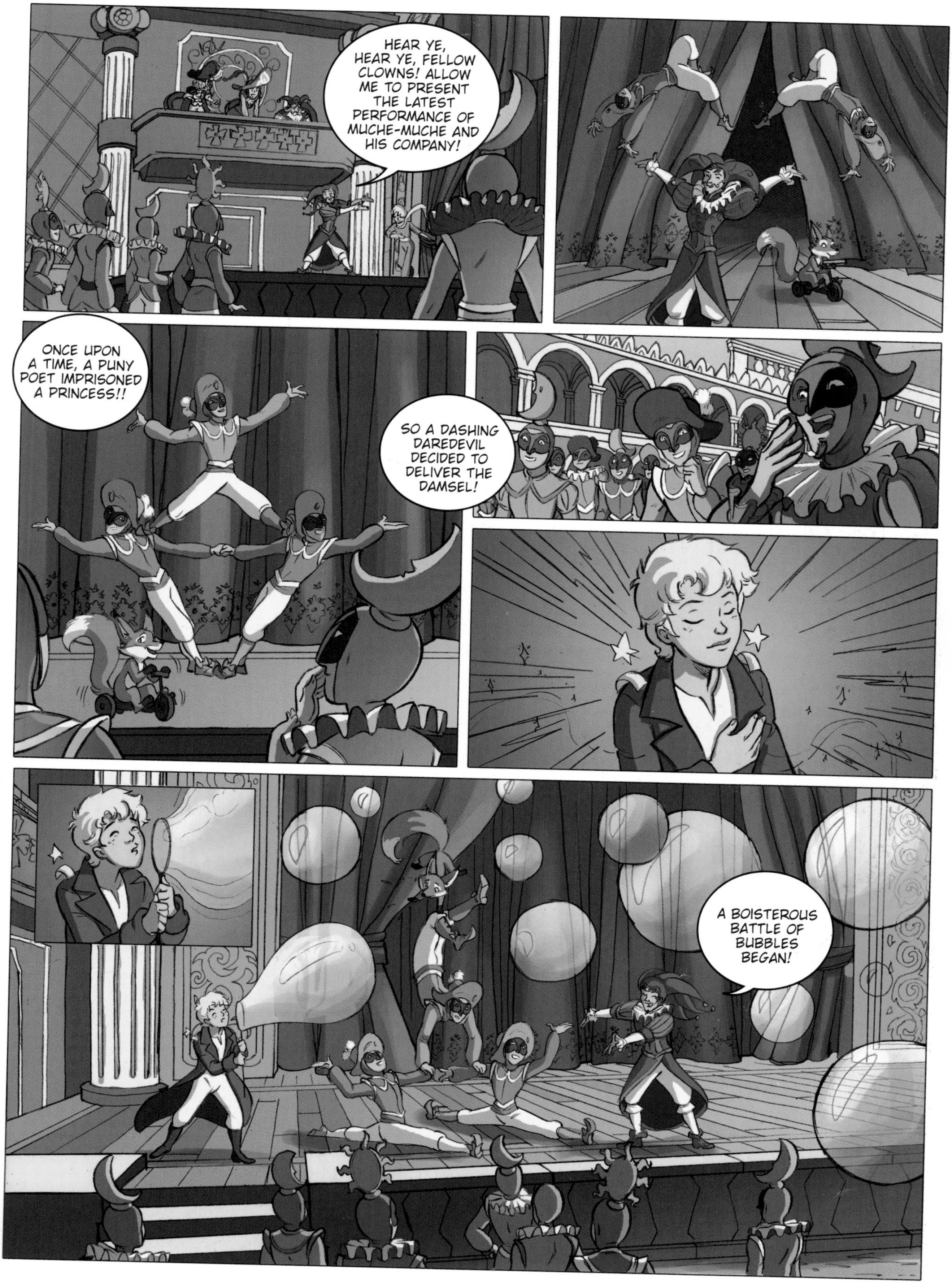
HEAR YE, HEAR YE, FELLOW CLOWNS! ALLOW ME TO PRESENT THE LATEST PERFORMANCE OF MUCHE-MUCHE AND HIS COMPANY!
ONCE UPON A TIME, A PUNY POET IMPRISONED A PRINCESS!!
SO A DASHING DAREDEVIL DECIDED TO DELIVER THE DAMSEL!
A BOISTEROUS BATTLE OF BUBBLES BEGAN!

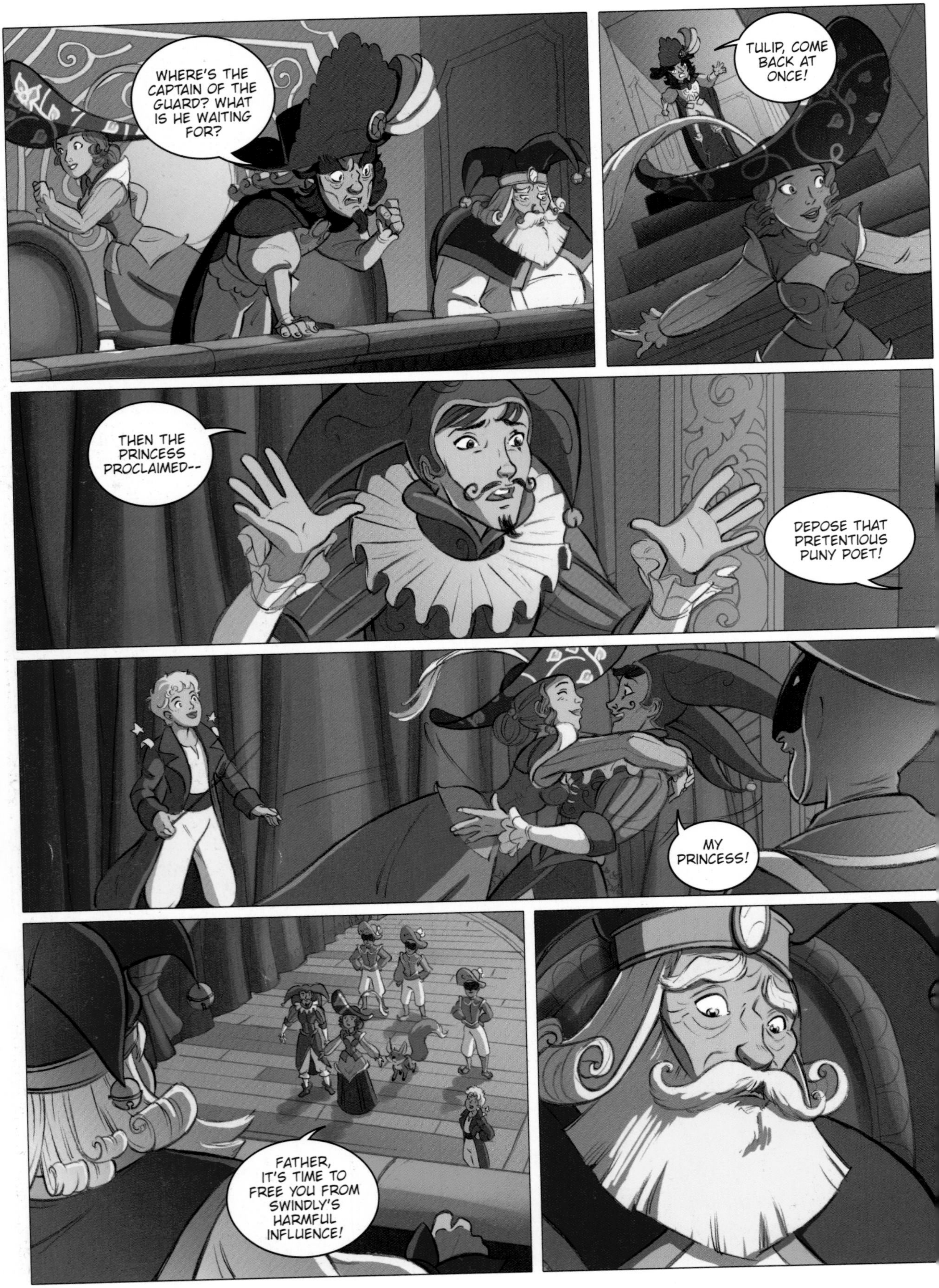
WHERE'S THE CAPTAIN OF THE GUARD? WHAT IS HE WAITING FOR?
TULIP, COME BACK AT ONCE!
THEN THE PRINCESS PROCLAIMED--
DEPOSE THAT PRETENTIOUS PUNY POET!
MY PRINCESS!
FATHER, IT'S TIME TO FREE YOU FROM SWINDLY'S HARMFUL INFLUENCE!

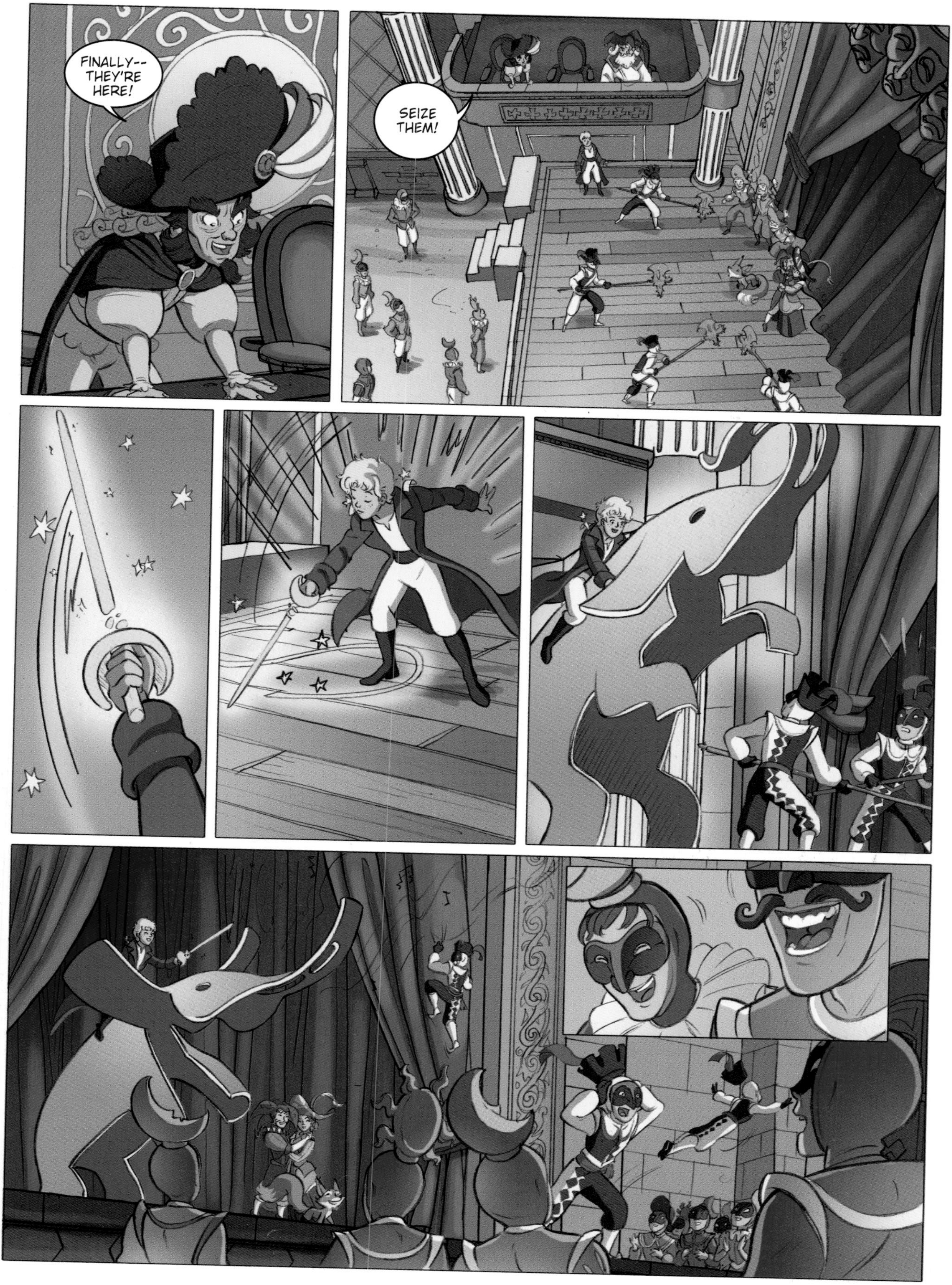
FINALLY-- THEY'RE HERE!
SEIZE THEM!

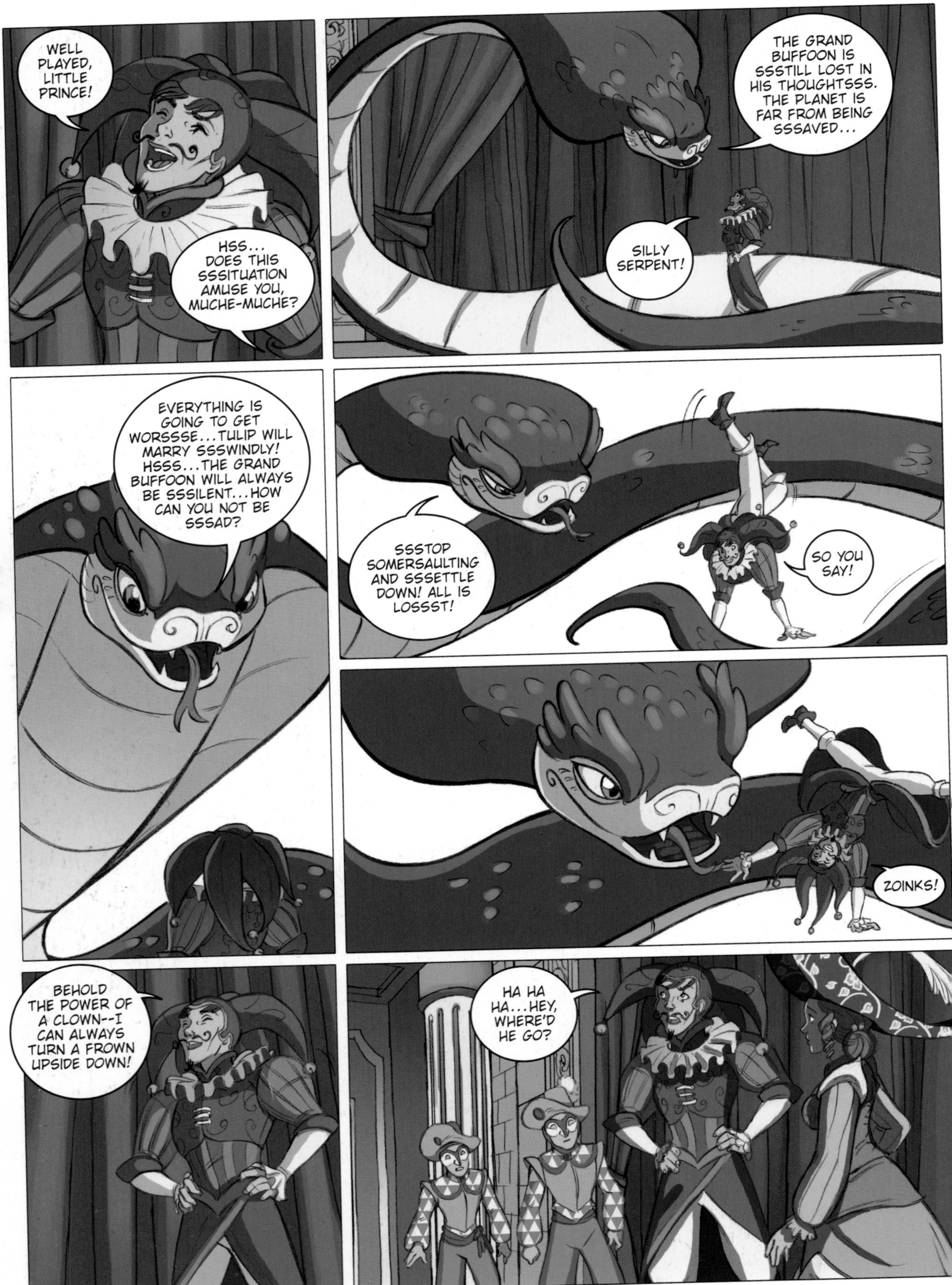
WELL PLAYED, LITTLE PRINCE!
HSS... DOES THIS SSSITUATION AMUSE YOU, MUCHE-MUCHE?
THE GRAND BUFFOON IS SSSTILL LOST IN HIS THOUGHTSSS. THE PLANET IS FAR FROM BEING SSSAVED...
SILLY SERPENT!
EVERYTHING IS GOING TO GET WORSSSE...TULIP WILL MARRY SSSWINDLY! HSSS...THE GRAND BUFFOON WILL ALWAYS BE SSSILENT...HOW CAN YOU NOT BE SSSAD?
SSSTOP SOMERSAULTING AND SSSETTLE DOWN! ALL IS LOSSST!
SO YOU SAY!
ZOINKS!
BEHOLD THE POWER OF A CLOWN--I CAN ALWAYS TURN A FROWN UPSIDE DOWN!
HA HA HA...HEY, WHERE'D HE GO?

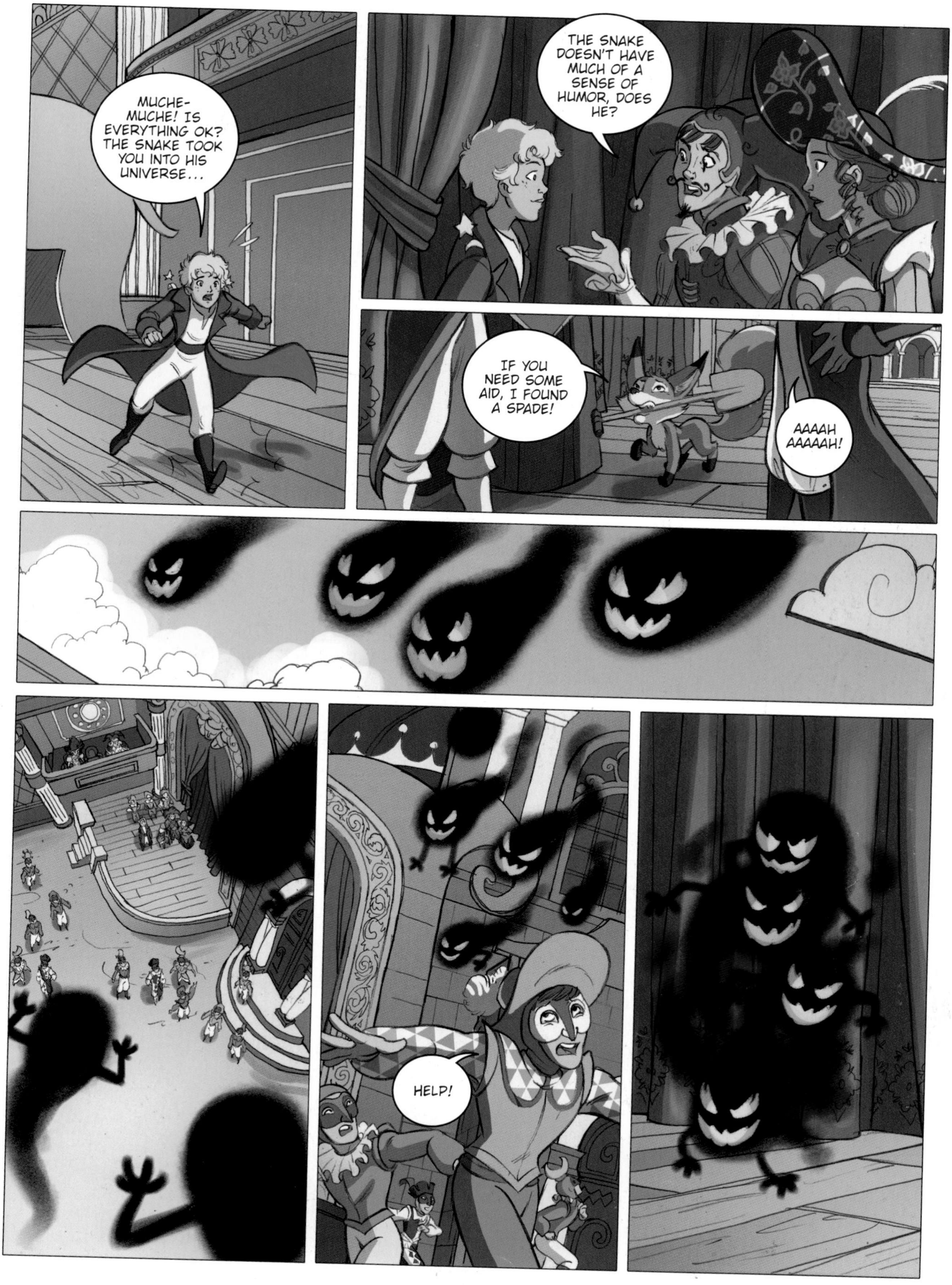
MUCHE-MUCHE! IS EVERYTHING OK? THE SNAKE TOOK YOU INTO HIS UNIVERSE...
THE SNAKE DOESN'T HAVE MUCH OF A SENSE OF HUMOR, DOES HE?
IF YOU NEED SOME AID, I FOUND A SPADE!
AAAAH AAAAAH!
HELP!

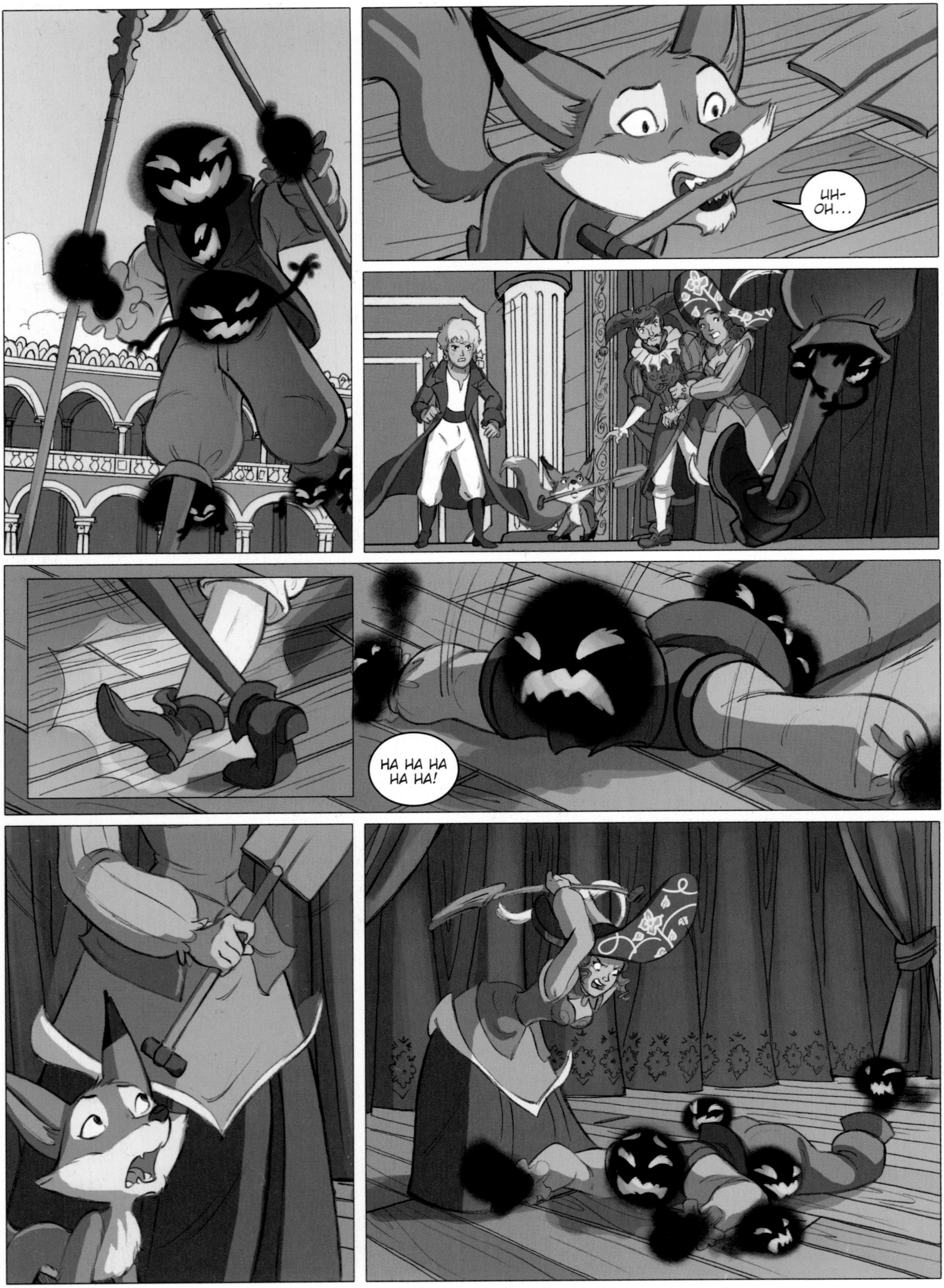
UH-
OH...
HA HA HA
HA HA!

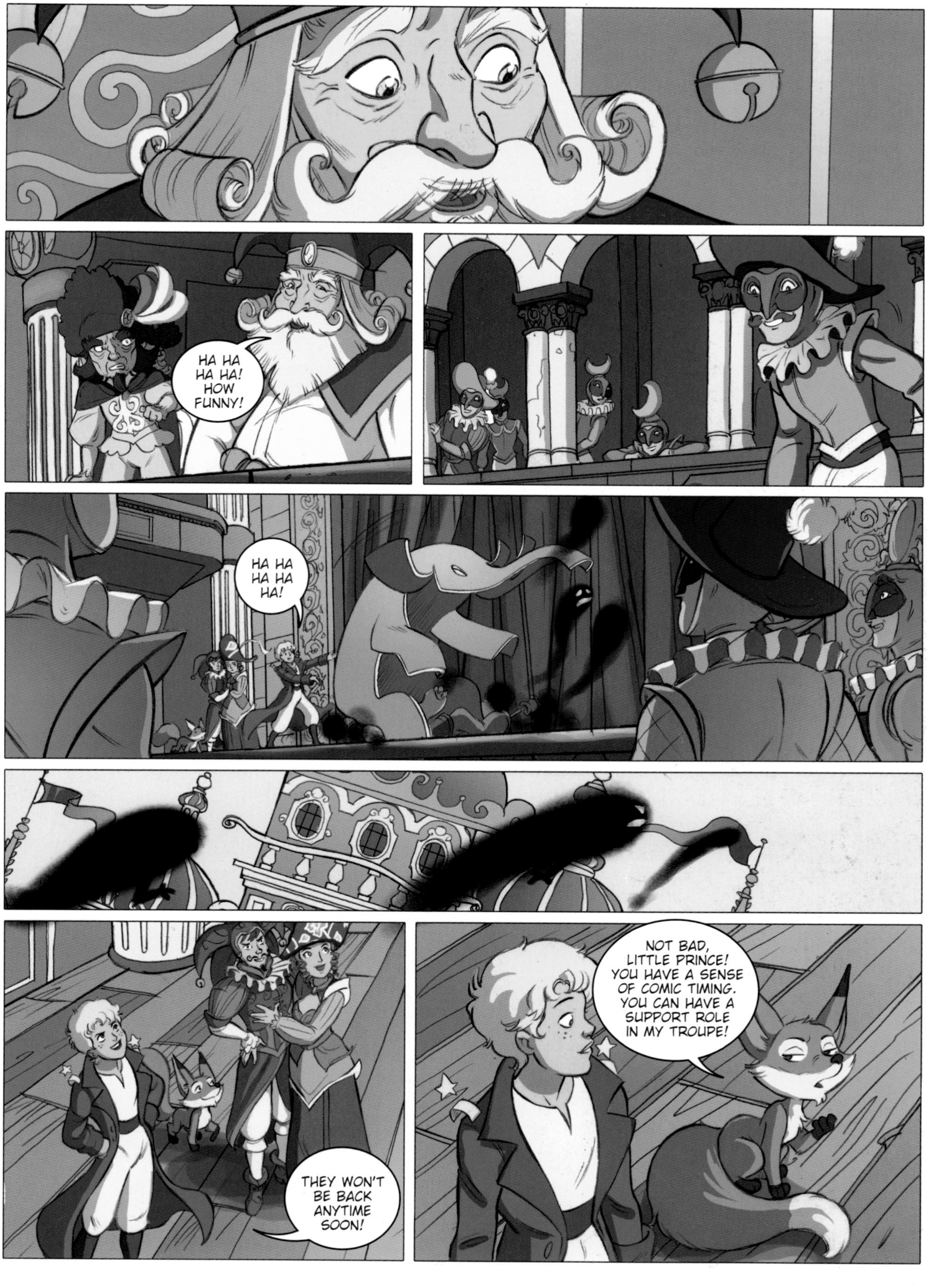
HA HA
HA HA!
HOW
FUNNY!
HA HA
HA HA
HA!
THEY WON'T
BE BACK
ANYTIME
SOON!
NOT BAD,
LITTLE PRINCE!
YOU HAVE A SENSE
OF COMIC TIMING.
YOU CAN HAVE A
SUPPORT ROLE
IN MY TROUPE!

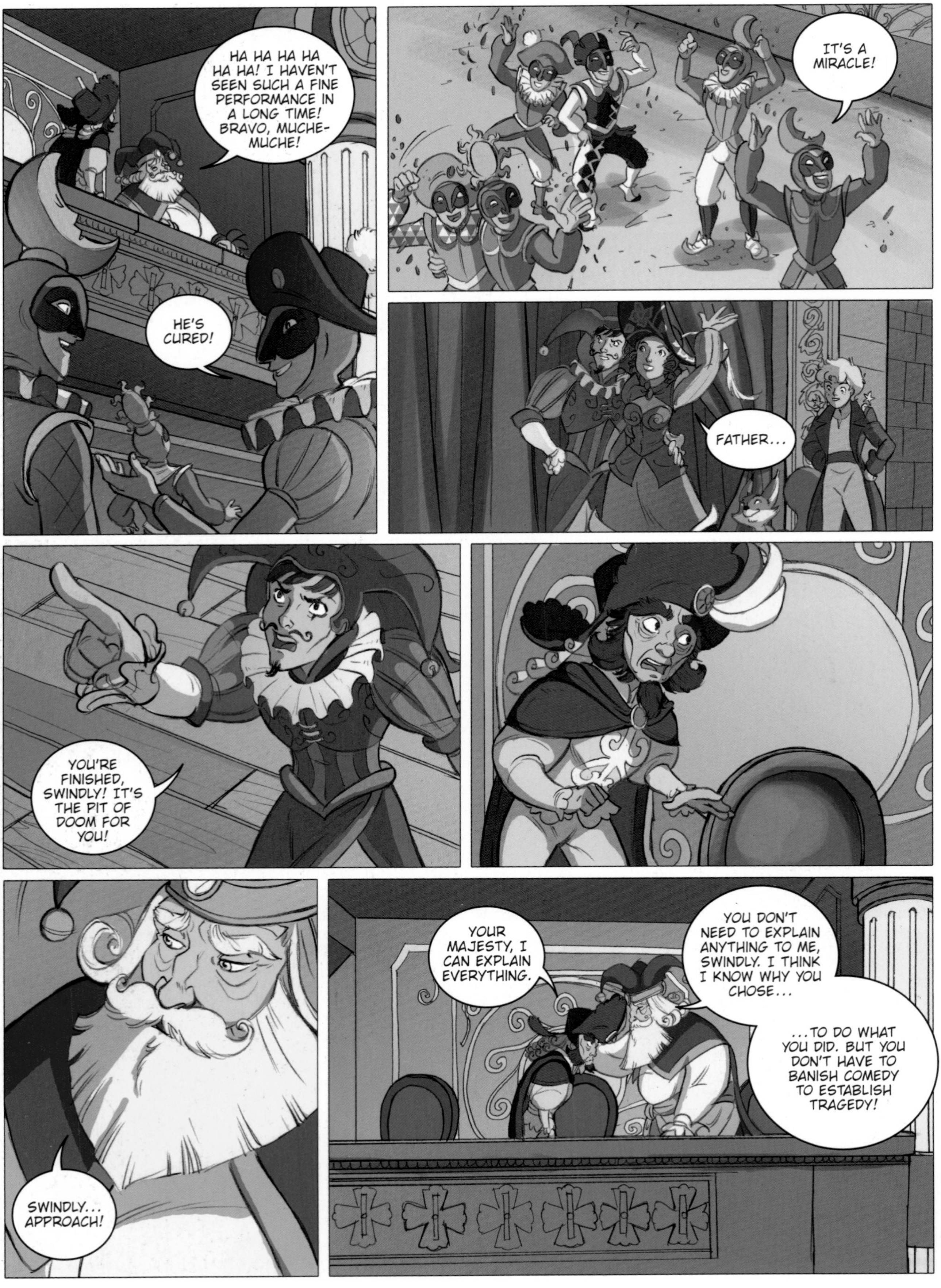
HA HA HA HA HA HA! I HAVEN'T SEEN SUCH A FINE PERFORMANCE IN A LONG TIME! BRAVO, MUCHE-MUCHE!
HE'S CURED!
IT'S A MIRACLE!
FATHER...
YOU'RE FINISHED, SWINDLY! IT'S THE PIT OF DOOM FOR YOU!
SWINDLY... APPROACH!
YOUR MAJESTY, I CAN EXPLAIN EVERYTHING.
YOU DON'T NEED TO EXPLAIN ANYTHING TO ME, SWINDLY. I THINK I KNOW WHY YOU CHOSE...
...TO DO WHAT YOU DID. BUT YOU DON'T HAVE TO BANISH COMEDY TO ESTABLISH TRAGEDY!

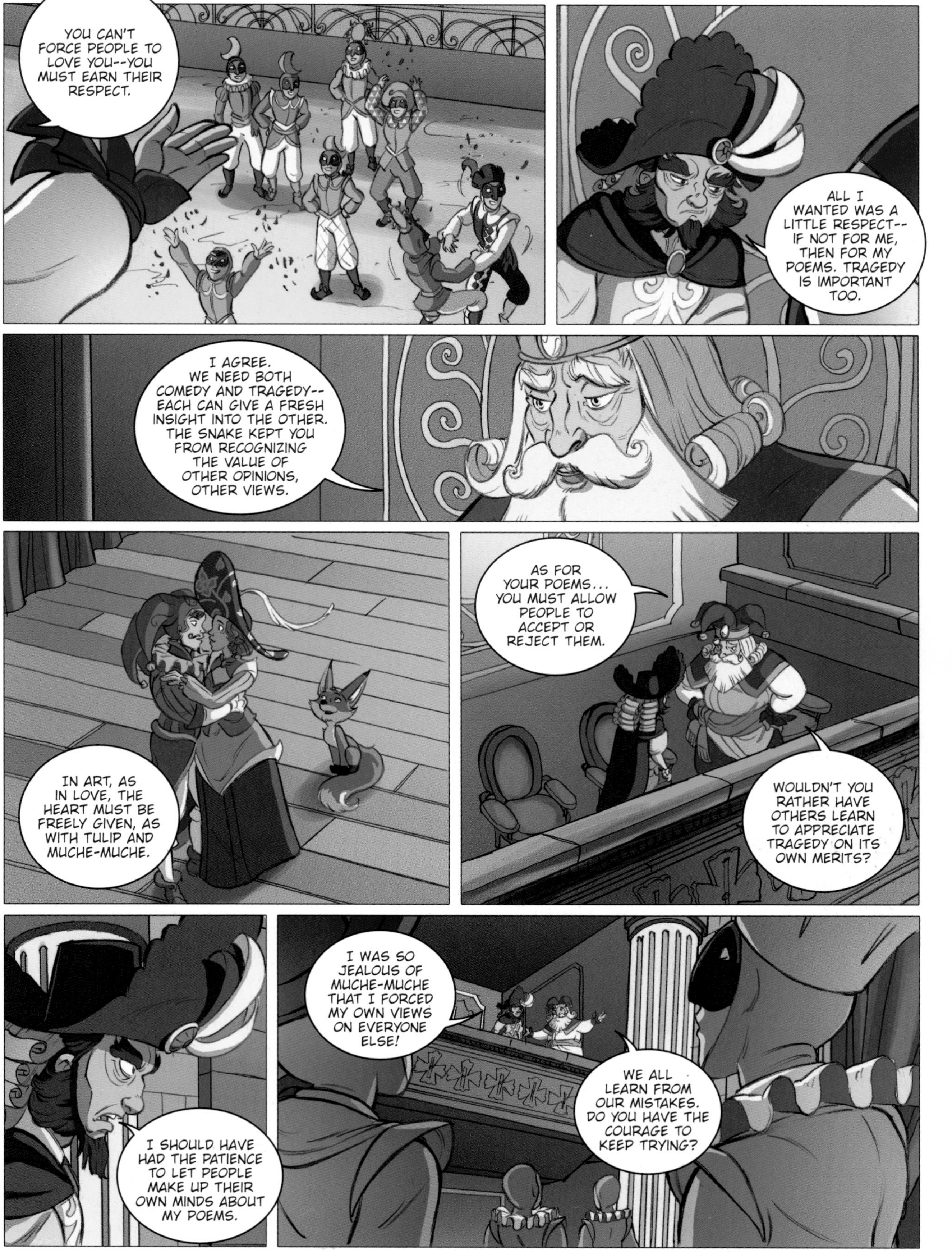
YOU CAN'T FORCE PEOPLE TO LOVE YOU--YOU MUST EARN THEIR RESPECT.
ALL I WANTED WAS A LITTLE RESPECT--IF NOT FOR ME, THEN FOR MY POEMS. TRAGEDY IS IMPORTANT TOO.
I AGREE. WE NEED BOTH COMEDY AND TRAGEDY--EACH CAN GIVE A FRESH INSIGHT INTO THE OTHER. THE SNAKE KEPT YOU FROM RECOGNIZING THE VALUE OF OTHER OPINIONS, OTHER VIEWS.
IN ART, AS IN LOVE, THE HEART MUST BE FREELY GIVEN, AS WITH TULIP AND MUCHE-MUCHE.
AS FOR YOUR POEMS... YOU MUST ALLOW PEOPLE TO ACCEPT OR REJECT THEM.
WOULDN'T YOU RATHER HAVE OTHERS LEARN TO APPRECIATE TRAGEDY ON ITS OWN MERITS?
I SHOULD HAVE HAD THE PATIENCE TO LET PEOPLE MAKE UP THEIR OWN MINDS ABOUT MY POEMS.
I WAS SO JEALOUS OF MUCHE-MUCHE THAT I FORCED MY OWN VIEWS ON EVERYONE ELSE!
WE ALL LEARN FROM OUR MISTAKES. DO YOU HAVE THE COURAGE TO KEEP TRYING?

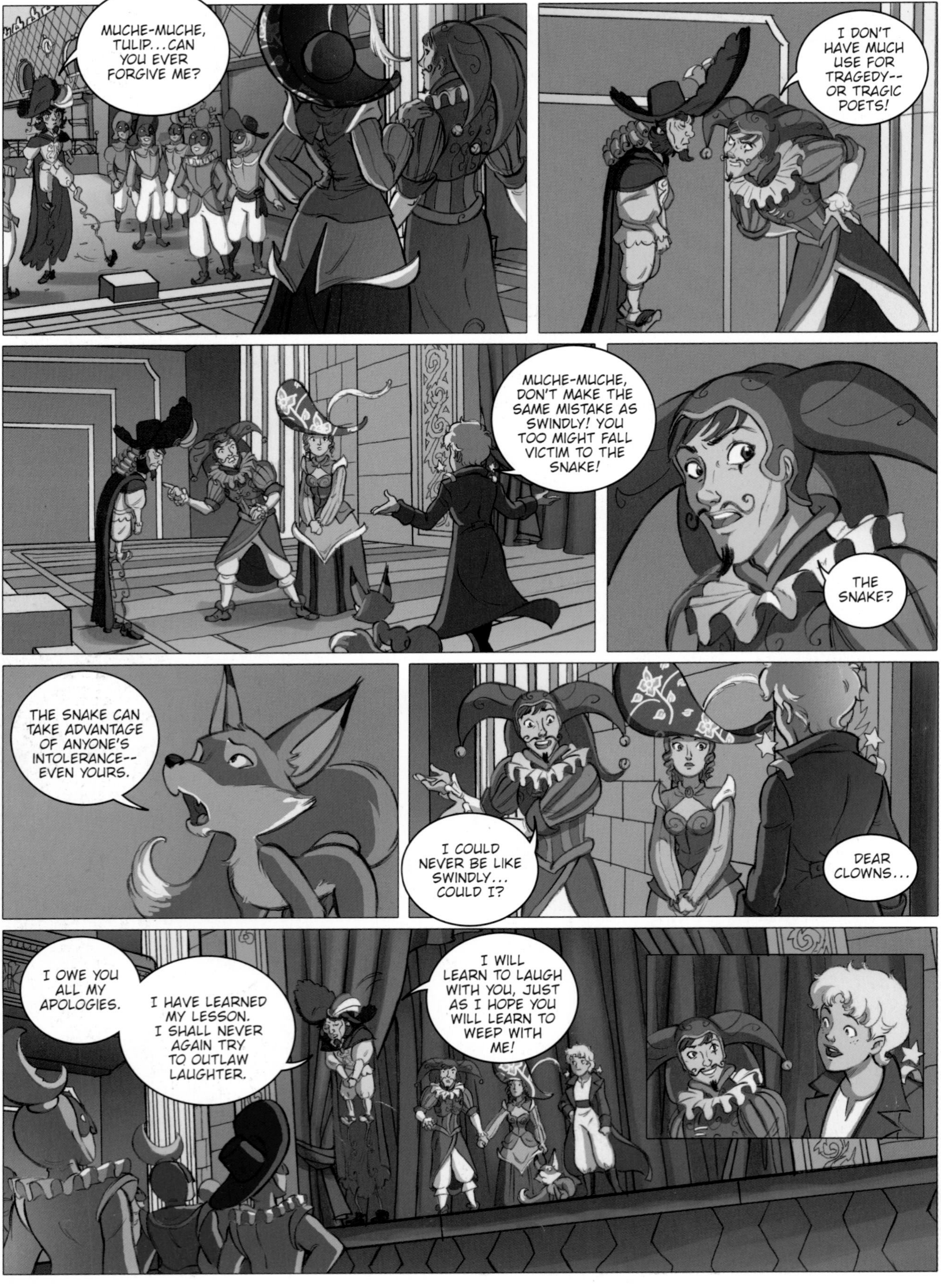
MUCHE-MUCHE, TULIP...CAN YOU EVER FORGIVE ME?
I DON'T HAVE MUCH USE FOR TRAGEDY-- OR TRAGIC POETS!
MUCHE-MUCHE, DON'T MAKE THE SAME MISTAKE AS SWINDLY! YOU TOO MIGHT FALL VICTIM TO THE SNAKE!
THE SNAKE?
THE SNAKE CAN TAKE ADVANTAGE OF ANYONE'S INTOLERANCE-- EVEN YOURS.
I COULD NEVER BE LIKE SWINDLY... COULD I?
DEAR CLOWNS...
I OWE YOU ALL MY APOLOGIES.
I HAVE LEARNED MY LESSON. I SHALL NEVER AGAIN TRY TO OUTLAW LAUGHTER.
I WILL LEARN TO LAUGH WITH YOU, JUST AS I HOPE YOU WILL LEARN TO WEEP WITH ME!

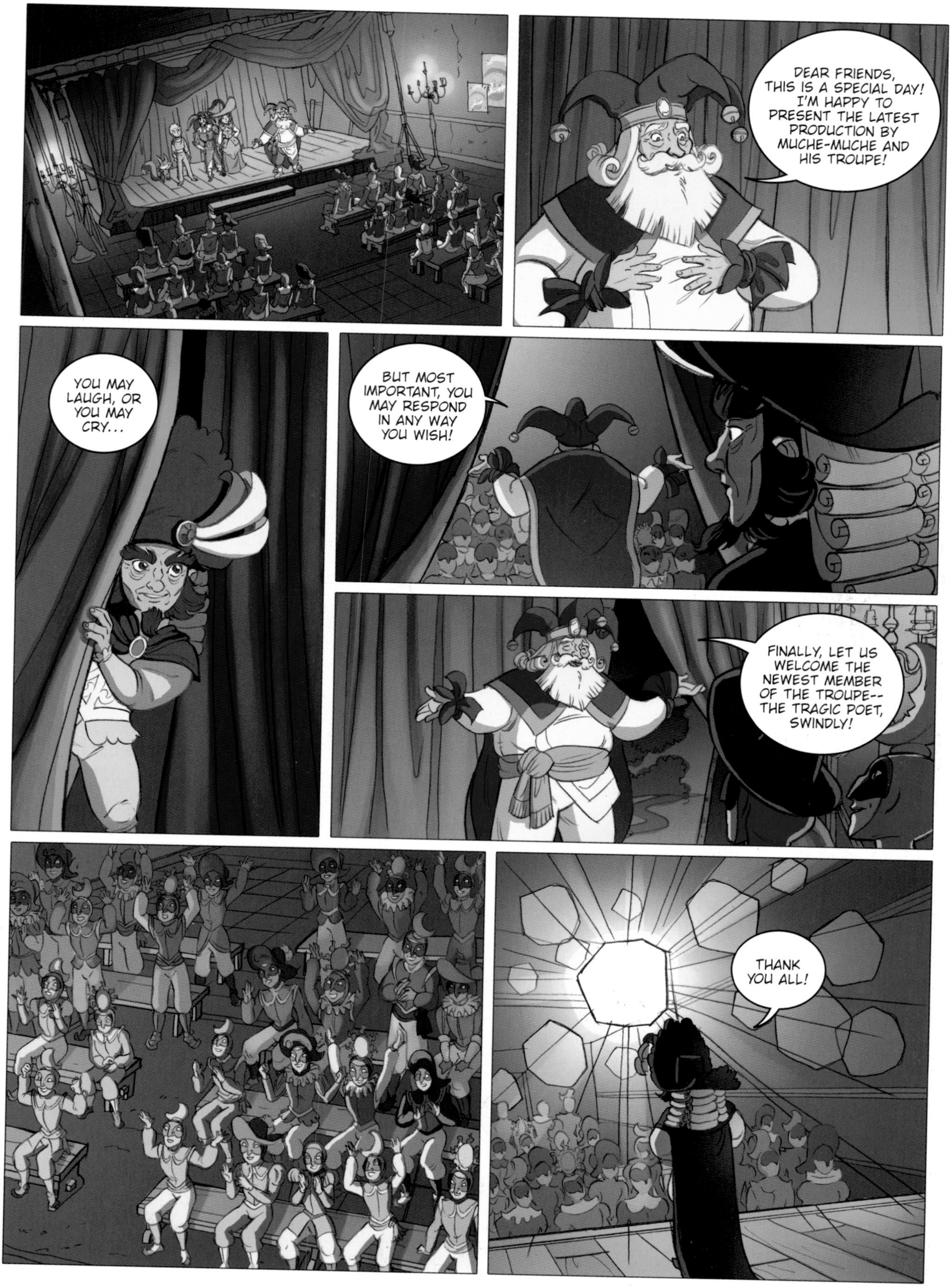
DEAR FRIENDS, THIS IS A SPECIAL DAY! I'M HAPPY TO PRESENT THE LATEST PRODUCTION BY MUCHE-MUCHE AND HIS TROUPE!
YOU MAY LAUGH, OR YOU MAY CRY...
BUT MOST IMPORTANT, YOU MAY RESPOND IN ANY WAY YOU WISH!
FINALLY, LET US WELCOME THE NEWEST MEMBER OF THE TROUPE-- THE TRAGIC POET, SWINDLY!
THANK YOU ALL!

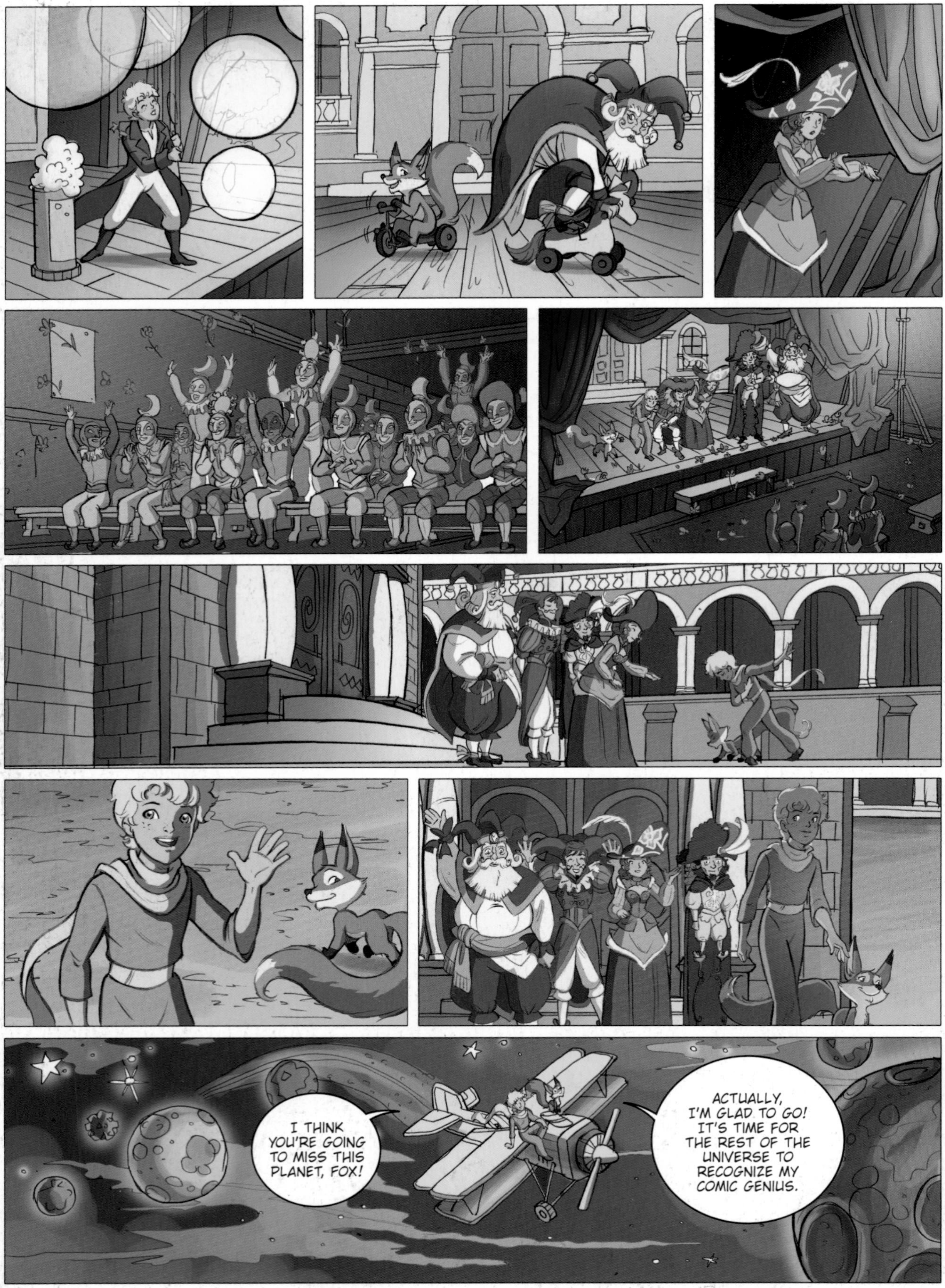
I THINK YOU'RE GOING TO MISS THIS PLANET, FOX!
ACTUALLY, I'M GLAD TO GO! IT'S TIME FOR THE REST OF THE UNIVERSE TO RECOGNIZE MY COMIC GENIUS.

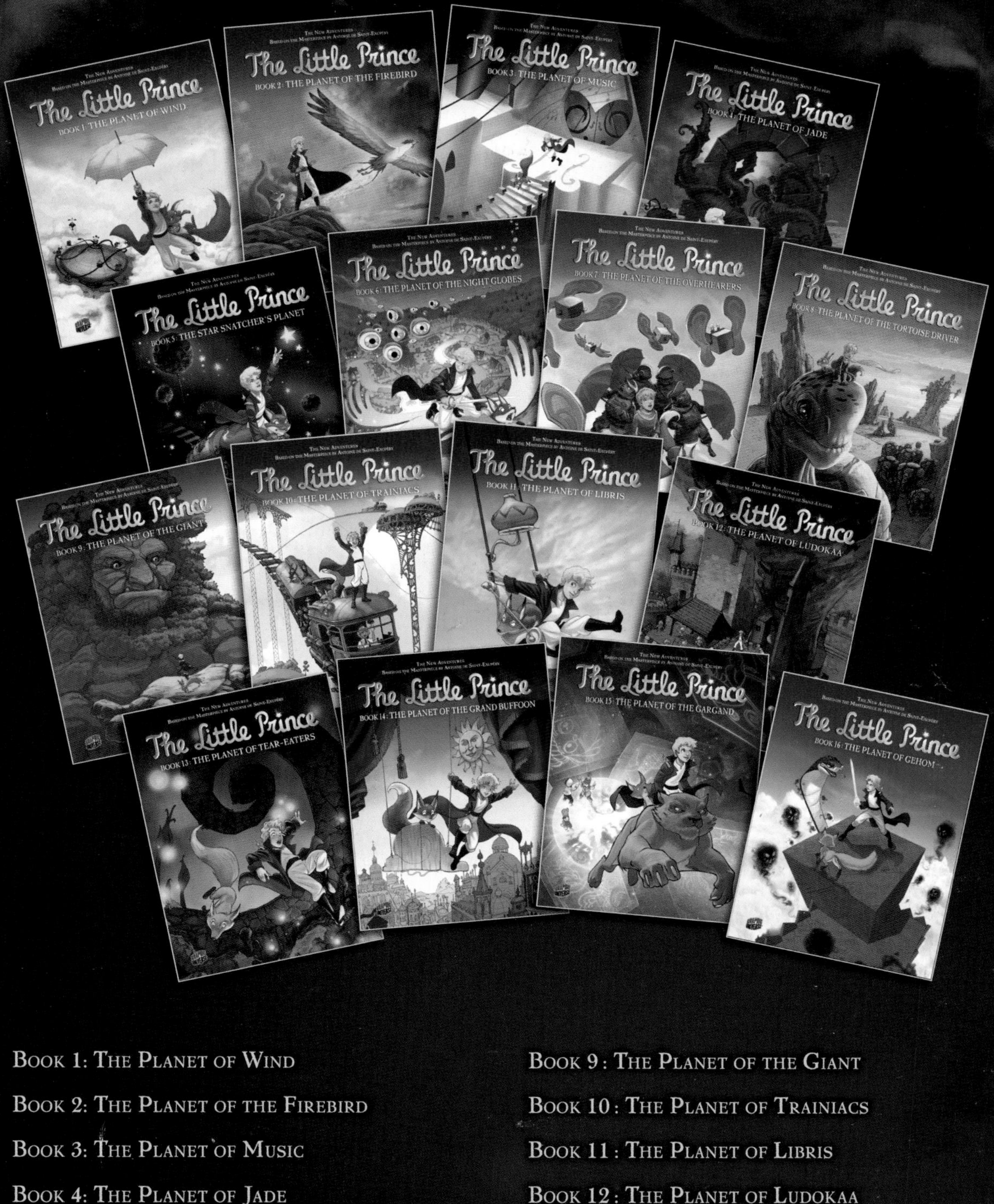
The Little Prince
BOOK 1: THE PLANET OF WIND
The Little Prince
BOOK 2: THE PLANET OF THE FIREBIRD
The Little Prince
BOOK 3: THE PLANET OF MUSIC
The Little Prince
THE PLANET OF JADE
The Little Prince
BOOK 5: THE STAR SNATCHER'S PLANET
The Little Prince
BOOK 6: THE PLANET OF THE NIGHT GLOBES
The Little Prince
BOOK 7: THE PLANET OF THE OVERHEARERS
The Little Prince
BOOK 8: THE PLANET OF THE TORTOISE DRIVER
The Little Prince
BOOK 9: THE PLANET OF THE GIANT
The Little Prince
BOOK 10: THE PLANET OF TRAINIACS
The Little Prince
THE PLANET OF LIBRIS
The Little Prince
BOOK 12: THE PLANET OF LUDOKAA
The Little Prince
BOOK 13: THE PLANET OF TEAR-EATERS
The Little Prince
BOOK 14: THE PLANET OF THE GRAND BUFFOON
The Little Prince
BOOK 15: THE PLANET OF THE GARGAND
The Little Prince
BOOK 16: THE PLANET OF GEHOM

Book 1: The Planet of Wind

Book 2: The Planet of the Firebird

Book 3: The Planet of Music

Book 4: The Planet of Jade

Book 5: The Star Snatcher's Planet

Book 6: The Planet of the Night Globes

Book 7: The Planet of the Overhearers

Book 8: The Planet of the Tortoise Driver

Book 9 : The Planet of the Giant

Book 10 : The Planet of Trainiacs

Book 11 : The Planet of Libris

Book 12 : The Planet of Ludokaa

Book 13 : The Planet of Tear-Eaters

Book 14 : The Planet of the Grand Buffoon

Book 15 : The Planet of the Gargand

Book 16 : The Planet of Gehom

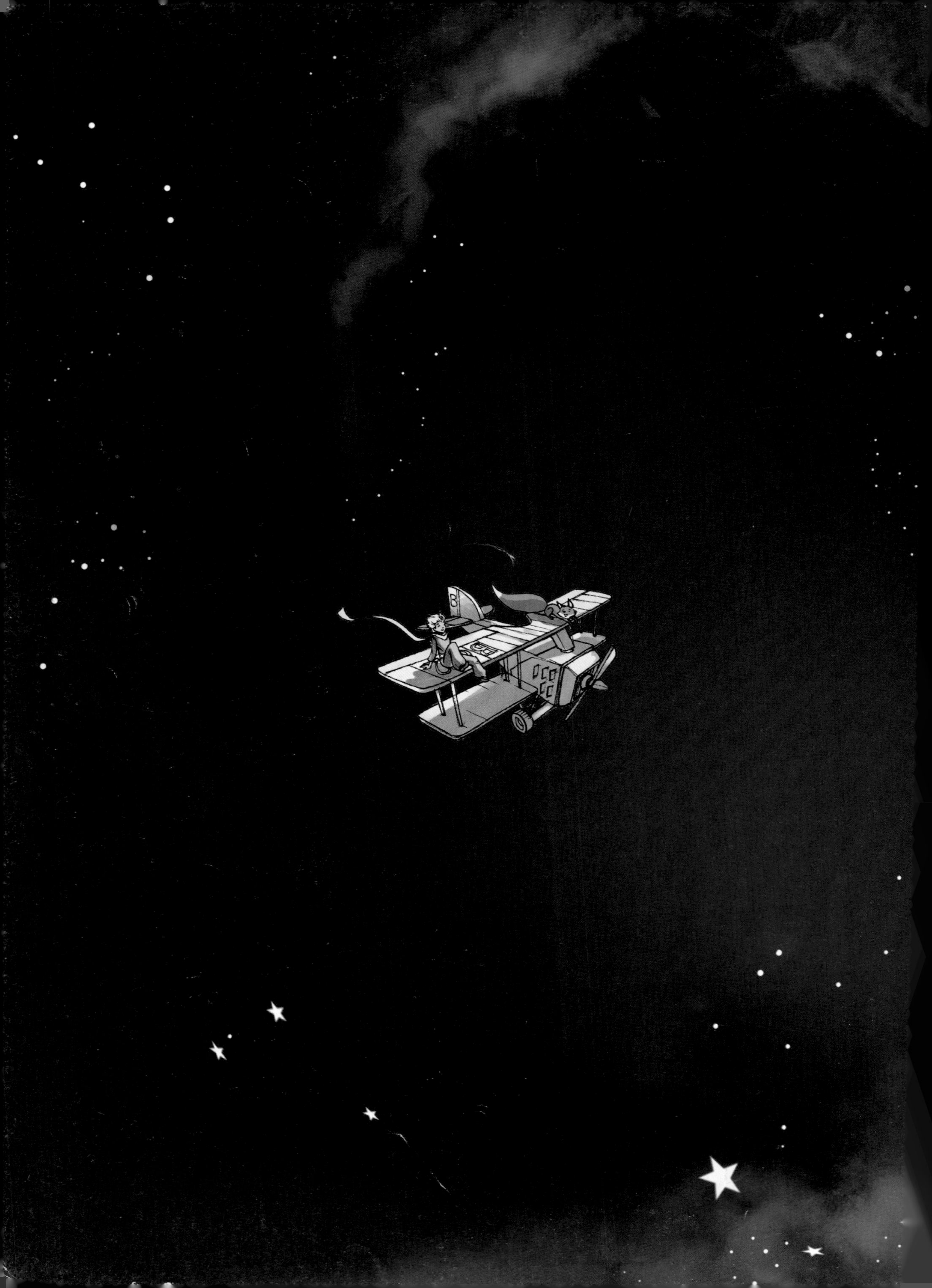

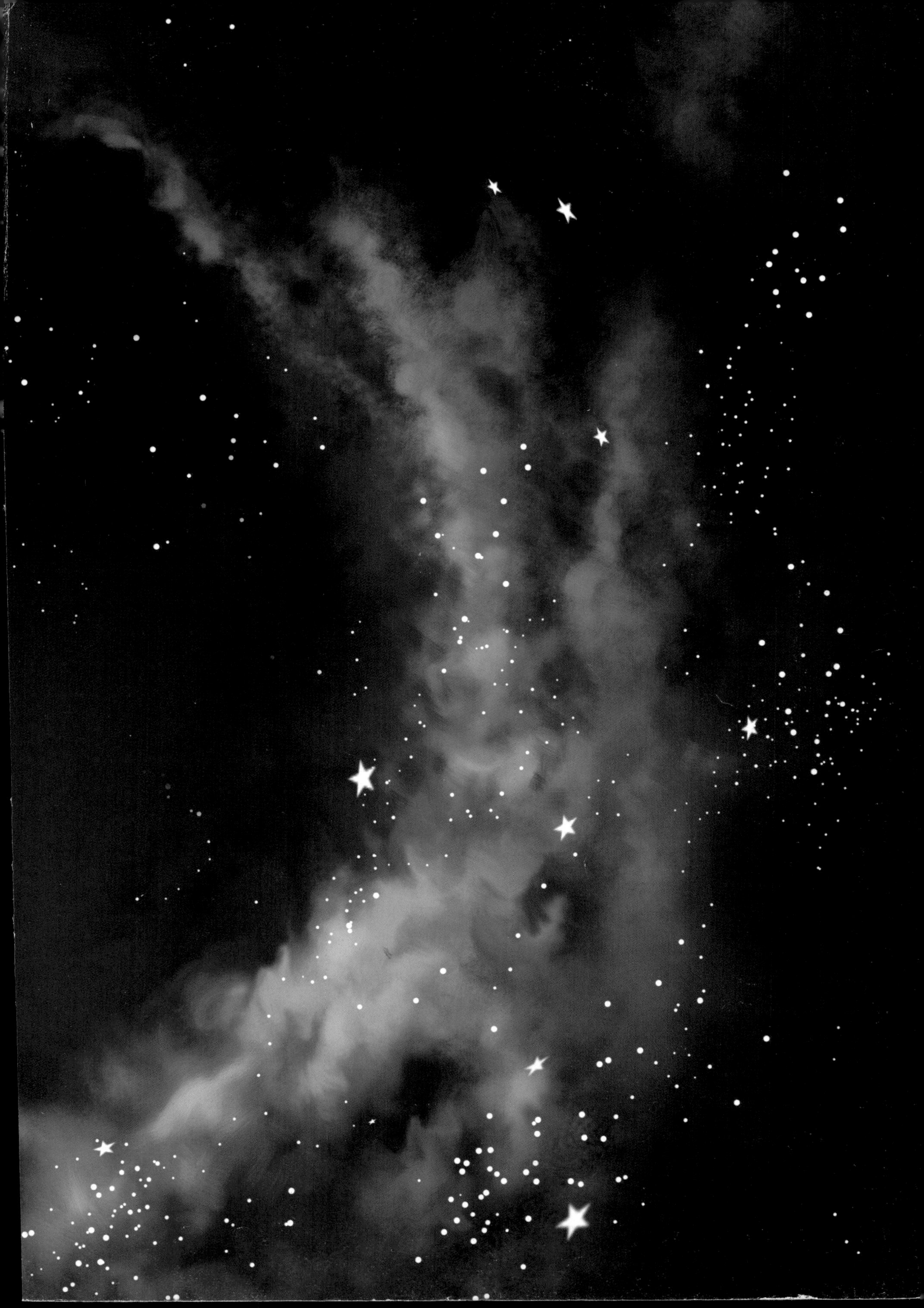